I0787577

Winternight

Winternight

Mythologia

Book 1

Jared N. Michaud

Winternight
Mythologia — Book 1

©2024 Jared N. Michaud
https://e6universe.com

All rights reserved. No portion of this story may be reproduced, stored in a retrieval system, or transmitted in any form or by any means—electronic, mechanical, photocopy, recording, scanning, or other—except for brief quotations in critical reviews or articles, without the prior written permission of the author.

Author's Note: This story is a work of fiction. Names, characters, places, and incidents are either products of the author's imagination or used fictitiously. All characters are fictional, and any similarity to people living or dead is purely coincidental.

ISBN: 978-1-965598-06-1 ebook
ISBN: 978-1-965598-05-4 paperback
ISBN: 978-1-965598-07-8 audiobook

Cover Art
Dave Evans
https://ccworkfloor.artstation.com/

Interior Design
Jared N. Michaud
https://www.jarednmichaud.com

Other Works
by Jared N. Michaud

Energematrice6
    Brightstar
    From the Void
    The Vale of Mysteries (Forthcoming)

Mythologia
    Winternight
    Il Alka E'Talania (Forthcoming)

Free Ebooks!
(And Value4Value)

The entire Energematrice6 library is available for free in ebook form at https://www.e6universe.com.

I offer this to you primarily because as a young person I wasn't able to afford to buy books, and was limited to what I could find at the library or, as I grew into my teens, online.

Please take advantage of it! Read everything!

If you enjoy my writing, I would appreciate it if you can return some value to me by buying something (like a physical book) to say "thank you" when you're able.

I hope you enjoy the world of Winternight!

For Christ, who will always be my hero.

Acknowledgments

This is not a new story. Winternight was originally written in 2008, and much of my memory from that era is lost in the mists of time. Thus, there are inevitably people to thank that I have completely forgotten about.

I always hate seeing authors apologize for things like this. Except when it's me in the hot seat, I really do appreciate every single contribution and I will feel terrible upon the (equally inevitable) discovery that I have, indeed, forgotten someone.

Thank you all. I appreciate every single one of you.

To Mary—As always, my wife (and best friend) was the first to support me in writing this story. You've always been the first to say that I need to pursue the things I love. Thank you.

To my beta-reader-in-chief, Nick—I genuinely didn't expect your passion for this story. It's always gratifying to see what strikes you about each manuscript. You, more than anyone else, convinced me that resurrecting this story was worth it. Thank you.

To my lore collector, Multaan—Despite the fact that your time is at a premium, you somehow keep finding more to help me out. Thank you.

To Luke—Your thoroughness and eye for detail are always appreciated. I wasn't sure I even needed beta readers for this one. Some of the points you made proved to me that I did. Thank you.

To Natalie—With every book I release, you contribute more and more. Having *you* find corrections for *my* grammar or spelling makes me smile every single time. Thank you.

To Dave—Finding a cover artist who can capture what I've aimed at with my books is almost as difficult as finding an editor who I can trust. You've done an excellent job. Thank you.

To all of the folks who contributed in some way to this story over fifteen years ago when I first wrote it, thank you as well. As ever, here's to many more years and many more stories.

Finally and always, to the Father of the heavenly lights in whom I find my life and breath and meaning. No thanks can be enough.

On Winter's night of power,
the comrades first shall meet.
The princess of the woodlands,
the scion of watchmen bright,
The child of dwarves and fairies,
the giant from the east,
The son of fallen Simia,
the outcast from the pack,
The wizard of the shattered coast,
though present yet unseen.
Together will they forge man's fate,
together stand against the storm,
For when they find the light of yore,
shall ancient darkness wake once more.

Prologue

The inn nestled among the giant trees of the forest; its seasoned timbers and weathered stone a reminder of old times and old storms, now long gone and forgotten. The black of night pressed close to the ancient structure; its thatch covered in a heavy blanket of fine, white snow. The snow still fell, and despite the canopy of surrounding trees the wind whipped it about until its descent was more horizontal than vertical at times. It was the sort of night in which finding shelter was the first concern of anyone unlucky enough to be caught in the raging storm.

Inside, a fire crackled brightly in the hearth, its orange hues vivid against the dingy backdrop of soot-stained plaster walls and the dark furniture of the common room. The room, however, was far warmer than the wind which, as if to prove the point, howled around the eaves and across the chimney. Several groups of guests huddled around the room, talking little and laughing not at all. A wary, oppressive silence hung about the place, making conversation seem an uneasy business at best, despite how much busier the inn was than usual.

An old man sat at a table by the fire in a rickety wooden chair, dozing with his long, white beard on his chest, and a tobacco-stained pipe hanging loose in his jaws. The other occupants unlucky enough to be caught in the storm, travelers all, huddled in small groups whispering among themselves occasionally.

Only a few were unusual enough to catch the eye. Three trolls sprawled at a low table in one corner, watching the room with hooded eyes, while in the opposite corner, by the door, a lone figure reclined, feet propped on a chair with the hood of a finely-woven cloak pulled low over his eyes. The rest of the patrons were obviously locals—their clothing homespun, their features weathered.

By the hearth the old man shifted, making his chair creak just as the wind gave an especially loud howl. Awakened by the noise, he started, then shivered uneasily and looked around as the wind howled again. He sighed and started to close his eyes again, but the door opened, letting in a blast of freezing air and snow. A moment later three cloaked figures stepped through, stamping the snow off their boots and closing the door behind them. Heads turned as people sought the source of the cold, but a moment later attention returned to their own various companies. Even newcomers didn't rouse much curiosity.

As the scant conversation resumed, two of the inn's occupants seemed to shrink back into the darkness in the corner furthest from the door. The three newcomers, their faces hidden in the shadows of their cloaks, conferred for a moment then picked their way through the room to where the old man sat watching them with a half-open eye. When they reached his table they stopped with the tallest of the three facing him, the other two flanking their leader, their eyes raking the occupants of the room.

The leader spoke, his voice low. "May we sit down, old one?"

The old man considered for a moment, then asked, "Who claims your sword, stranger?"

The three shifted away from the table a bit and the leader sneered, "That is a dangerous question, old one."

The old man shrugged. "Age teaches one not to fear questions... This inn is a freehold. Sit where you like." The leader nodded and the three quickly seated themselves in the remaining chairs around the old man's table, their motions fluid.

The old man seemed about to speak but their leader asked, "What news is there in this place?"

The old man stared into the fire for a moment; putting up a hand to stroke his beard, then chuckled. "You ask dangerous questions, dark one. ...But news? ...I don't know that there is news...though..." He twitched his shoulders in a shrug. "There are always stories."

"Yes?" The newcomer's voice, still low, had taken on a sharper quality, and his eyes shone with shocking brilliance from the depths of his hood, seeming to bore into the old man, who raised his bushy eyebrows, looking faintly amused.

"Rumor has war in the south. They say the king of Trusk has sworn vengeance upon the Jahazi trolls of the great plain. There was something about a lost hunting party I think, but I don't pay much attention to such. By the time the news gets here, it's almost as old as I am." He made a throwaway gesture with the hand that was not holding his pipe.

The newcomer scanned the room again. "I see," he murmured, sounding faintly disappointed.

The old man turned his eyes again upon the leader, and this time his voice had a slight edge. "Now tell me—who claims your sword, stranger?"

One of the man's companions cursed and reached for his belt, but the leader raised a hand to halt him. "You will do yourself harm, old one. You must know that men are killed for asking another's allegiance. The Oath is both enemy and friend to any of us. Still..." He shrugged. "My sword is my own. I owe no allegiance."

"In that case..." the old man fixed his gaze on the newcomer's face, still hidden in the strange shadows of his hood, as if seeking a reaction. "There are rumors of strange doings in the mountains as well."

"Doings?" The stranger's voice regained its odd note and he resumed his former, piercing stare.

The old man shrugged. "They say were-men have been seen in the north holds. They say a deep shadow has fallen over the mountains, gathering up all the dark things of the netherworld. If the rumors are true, the creatures hide there, awaiting their master's return so they can claim the world for their own. And, for those who believe such things, they say the Star of Yore shines once more."

The stranger hissed, the sound of a long breath drawn in between clenched teeth and said, half in question, half in demand, "Who has told you such tales? What do you know?"

The old man hesitated. "Well..." Then he shook his head as if pushing an idea away. "No," he muttered under his breath. Then he reiterated a little louder, "No," as if he had decided some question in his own mind.

The stranger seized his arm. "What have you heard? Tell me."

The old man paused and stared pointedly at the stranger's hand, which clutched demandingly at his arm. In response, the hand was slowly withdrawn and the old man turned his gaze to the fire once again, saying nothing for a long moment.

When he next spoke, his voice was distant, as if he pondered a place far away or a time long past. "T'was a traveler who told me; a strange man who seemed to wear the silence as a cloak. He shared my fire for a night. I have never heard the like of the tale he told, even from of old. … It seems fanciful beyond belief. Such fancies are too big a mouthful for this modern world, when children no longer believe even in were-men or giants." He snorted softly. "But…" he twitched his shoulders in another shrug. "If he spoke true, we may see the signs of the ancient times once again."

His eyes unfocused slightly, and he seemed to be gazing inward for a moment to something unseen by the rest of the world. Then he began his story…

1

She stood motionless on the edge of the clearing, hood pulled low over her eyes, listening. The forest around her was as dark and still as she, the trees sending searching branches into the night. The moon above her shone bright above the woodland's canopy, which spread to the south and west as far as the eye could see. Very near to the north and sweeping around into the distance to the east, a wall of mountains rose huge and forbidding into the sky—strange, terrible fortresses of black stone guarded by dark, purplish clouds that swallowed up their peaks. Seen from the corner of the eye, the clouds seemed to creep farther and farther outward from the mountains as if they wished to consume the sky itself. If one turned to look at them directly, however, they still hovered there, churning slowly.

The wind stirred the trees, whispering through the branches and brushing lightly over the cloak shrouding the solitary figure on the hillside, still standing unmoving in the darkness.

There was something wrong with the air—with the night itself. Something was present that should not be there, she thought, or possibly something was missing. She wasn't certain and that in itself was a bad sign. She had walked the forests of Eschaton for far longer than anyone from the most of the world's races had ever lived. She knew the forests well—even this dark, unnatural one.

Again the breeze brought the scent of the woods to her nose, and again she sensed the almost imperceptible tang of bitterness—of something wrong. Yet, as she tried to isolate it in her mind, it disappeared again. Behind her the trees stirred, and she turned to see her companion emerge from their shadow. He stalked toward her, eyes flicking around the clearing.

"My lady Talina, the path ahead is clear. And..." his eyes swept the clearing again, uneasily. "Something is wrong with this wind."

"Yes, Bretran, I feel it. We must be getting close... perhaps closer than we'd like."

He frowned. "This is no time for second thoughts. If you would go back..."

"No, of course not." Talina waved her hand dismissively. "This is an uneasy night, and we haven't yet found..."

Bretran cut in, his hard face set itself into grim, determined lines that had become more and more familiar of late. "We must continue. That path is set now."

Suddenly, Talina's hand shot up and her head whipped to the right, toward the edge of the clearing. With her gesture, Bretran melted back into the shadows as if he had never been; his hand already moving to the hilt of his sword. Talina's breath hissed as she inhaled, then she turned and stepped quickly back into the forest.

The leaves on the trees, still but for the wind, began to tremble slightly, as if the earth were shaking imperceptibly.

It grew more and more as the seconds passed, and a sound came, faint at first then louder and louder, like thunder gathering in the distance and rolling in through the darkness. Then the thunder became a roar, and a shape broke through the trees on the southeastern side of the clearing.

It was moving impossibly fast, but its features were unmistakable, even in the dimness. It was a horse of a kind both beautiful and terrible. Its black coat shone with magic, and its mane streamed straight out behind it from the terrific speed at which it ran. Red lightning flashed in its eyes, and light danced around its hooves as if it struck sparks from the ground, whether it trod upon stones, grass, or the softest earth.

Talina had seen a Dread Steed once before, when she was very young, and this was a stallion of the kind that belonged only to the Fair Folk. It seemed to freeze for a moment before her eyes, and she caught a profile both noble and infinitely dangerous, perfect of form and limb, its rider seeming impossibly small upon its back.

Talina shrank even further back into the shadows as it thundered across the clearing, a blur of speed, hooves beating the earth. Behind it came the terrifying avalanche of the Wild Hunt, all hooves and whips and Fae lights, red and black leather flashing as it pounded past through the darkness. Along with the Dread Steeds came the Dark Hounds. They were creatures of nightmare, the larger cousins of the great forest wolves, bred magically for the Hunt, their eyes and teeth glittering as they followed fast on the heels of their masters' steeds.

Once it began, the parade of shapes and light and eyes racing through the gloom seemed to go on forever, and Talina stood absolutely still, barely breathing. Hundreds of horses and riders fairly flew through the clearing each moment, but they just kept coming. As Talina watched, the night was broken by a cry from the darkness and two shapes sailed out of the mass of horsemen to land rolling in the grass on the near side of the clearing.

Then, as quickly as the careening cavalcade had begun, it simply ended, and the ground was still, but for a little residual trembling that soon faded to nothing. There was no sign at all that the Hunt had passed. Not a blade of grass was bent, and the trees were as still and silent as ever. All that remained were two inert shapes, lying in the grass.

2

Talina stood absolutely still, watching. There was a good chance that when the leader of the Hunt realized he had lost two of his hunters he would return for them. The Folk were a reclusive lot, but for the Hunt and the Snatchers, and seeing even those was a rarity. They would not knowingly leave two of their own among the hostile outsiders...but the Folk were only human, just as any of the races of man. They were just as likely to err.

Seconds stretched into long, silent minutes as Talina waited, totally still but for her breathing. Finally, after what must have been a full quarter of an hour, one of the two figures before her stirred and moaned.

A moment later, it sat up and looked blearily around. In the silver light of the full moon, Talina could see it was a girl, and a rather tiny one (as would have been expected for the Folk). She would have been under four links high, standing upright. That was short even for one of the Folk.

She turned her head side-to-side for a moment, then gave a muffled cry and started toward the other figure, still sprawled across the damp grass of the clearing. As the girl moved forward to hover over the still form, Talina stepped silently from the trees.

Talina was a gray shadow in the silver moonlight of Winternight, moving through the clearing, her cloak's colors matching her surroundings with a little too much accuracy for the eye to be comfortable. Approaching the two, she could see that the one on the ground was a boy—and entirely too large for one of the Folk.

Talina let out a short, surprised hiss of breath and the girl whipped around, coming instantly from her knees into a defensive crouch over her companion, eyes shining in the moonlight.

Talina halted, surprised. Her little breath should not have been audible even a few links away. The girl made a grab for something inside her cloak and she seemed almost frantic as Talina raised a hand in something between greeting and caution.

"Who are you?" Uttered in a voice of tinkling silver bells, the girl's challenge was strong enough to carry clearly, and the warning in it was unmistakable, yet still soft enough not to be heard beyond the edge of the clearing. Talina's eyebrows rose. Such control and purpose were impressive considering the circumstances. That was especially true if this was only a child. It could be hard to tell with the folk.

"Peace, girl. I've nothing against you."

There was a noise of cracking brush from across the clearing and Bretran stepped from the shadow of the trees, his sword drawn. The girl whipped around, her hand coming out of her cloak to reveal a dagger, held cocked and ready to throw.

"Drop it." Bretran's words slammed into the still night like a granite boulder, and the girl hesitated, her arm still, staring across the clearing at the tall man, his chain mail gleaming dully under the moon, his sword an accusing finger of steel pointed straight at her.

The two held there, frozen for long moments until, slowly, the girl replaced the half-drawn knife within her cloak. Talina had moved silently up until she stood barely five links behind the Fae child and the Deegani boy. Deegani he was; Talina could see him clearly now, sprawled in a tangle of limbs across the grass, his chest rising and falling ever-so-slightly.

Talina spoke gently and the girl turned back to her. "What is your name, child of the Folk?"

"Cyrith." The girl stared suspiciously up at her, still hovering protectively over the unconscious boy on the ground. "What do you want?"

Talina raised an eyebrow. "From you? Likely nothing." Her eyes considered the Fae child for a long moment. "Would you have us leave you as we found you? Castoffs of the Hunt?"

Cyrith started to nod almost belligerently, then brought herself up short and looked down at the boy, who had begun to stir feebly. "I... I don't know."

The boy opened his eyes and Cyrith threw herself upon his neck, hugging him fiercely. "Oh, Malakai, are you all right?"

He groaned and reached out to hug her in return, then set her easily on her feet as he sat up. He was nearly as tall sitting as she was standing.

Seeing Talina, his eyes narrowed, but he remained silent, simply studying her for a long time. Talina returned his gaze, her face revealing nothing in the moonlight. There was a depth to his eyes, she saw. It was a depth that no child should have. It reminded her of...

Talina frowned as Bretran approached, interrupting her train of thought. He was still watching the children carefully, though he had sheathed his sword.

In a clipped, irritated voice he said, "What now? We can't take them with us—not there." He jerked a thumb toward the mountains to the north.

Talina raised her eyebrow. "Oh? We must take them with or send them back alone, and one is just as dangerous as the other."

Bretran nodded. "But what about..."

Talina raised a hand to stop him, an odd expression on her face. "Hold a moment." She turned to the boy. "Who are you?"

His slight frown was as thoughtful as his previous glance had been. "I am Malakai. Who might you be, my lady aylf?"

Talina frowned. Her kind were rare across Eschaton. She would never have expected one so young to recognize her, especially a Deegani. Using the formal 'Aylf' was yet another surprise. Most used the more common pronunciation of 'elf.' This boy was quite a puzzle. "I am Talina ne'al Kalin ni'al In'Kalith." Malakai nodded gravely and Talina thought she caught a glint of amusement in his eye.

Talina glanced to Bretran then turned and faced the two squarely. The Fae girl had moved to stand half behind the boy, obviously deferring to him. Though she remained silent as Talina spoke, her eyes never wavered.

"You may join us on our journey if you wish. We travel north to the mountains. Otherwise there is a town, Findale, three days south. We can give you food and water. If circumstances were different, we would accompany you, but we cannot."

At the word mountains, Malakai's eyes narrowed but he shook his head. "Please, don't leave us. This is a terrible place, dangerous to Folk, both Fair and Deep."

Talina's lips curved wryly. "The forest is dark, true, but the mountains are the source of the darkness. You would join us there?" Her tone was dry. "Safety lies to the south, boy, not in the Madra'risa."

Malakai shrugged as Cyrith shifted uncomfortably behind him. "Yet it is to the dark mountains that you travel, lady. Surely we would be safe with you?"

The neutrality of Talina's tone was its own sort of shrug. "Very well, come then. Our horses are over the hill." She motioned the children toward the southern edge of the clearing.

There were four horses. Two were common pack animals, only lightly burdened. The other two were saddled for riding and obviously far from ordinary. One was a mare. Her color, an odd, eye-twisting combination of gray and brown, seemed to fade into the foliage. The other was a pure white stallion, standing with head held high, intelligent eyes watching the trees suspiciously. It seemed he too disliked something about the place.

It was the work of moments to move the remainder of their supplies to a single packhorse and rig a makeshift bridle so the children could ride. They had to ride bareback, but it didn't seem to bother them. They clung to the horse and each other as if they had been born to it. After Talina mounted the mare and Bretran the stallion, the little party moved out toward the mountains. Talina led, sitting erect in the saddle, hood pulled low, alert to any change in the forest around her. Next were the children, holding onto the packhorse and saying little, staring into the woods as if they expected terrible creatures to plunge out of the brush at any moment and attack them. Bretran took up the rear, leading the remaining packhorse, his eyes flicking about, senses alert.

Talina headed them straight for the mountains that towered so near in the north, following a ghost of a path that was invisible to the others at times. As they rode the night seemed to wear on forever; the moon never moving from its place behind them; the entire world silent as the grave. Ahead, the mountains loomed ever closer, towering peaks still lost in the clouds.

It must have continued that way—the horses' hooves making little crunching sounds in the needles of the forest floor, the saddles creaking slightly—for several hours. Time, though, seemed to stand still. The breeze died, leaving the world frozen in the darkness, unmoving and silent.

3

As they continued, their surroundings became increasingly threatening. The trees' branches seemed to reach out for them, and the silence that had at first seemed merely eerie grew more and more ominous. All the while, Talina continued to catch stronger and stronger scent of whatever wrongness she had first become aware of in the clearing. Irritatingly, she still wasn't able to identify it.

After a long enough time to leave them all in a near trance, Talina spoke, breaking the spell the night had held them under. "How did a Deegani boy come to be in the company of the Fae? ...and riding the Hunt, no less?" She didn't turn her head, and after her voice faded, she might almost never have spoken.

A moment later Cyrith asked, "Why should we tell you anything?" Her voice was high and musical despite the belligerence of its message.

Seemingly ignoring her, Talina said, "Cyrith...an interesting name...what is your lineage, girl?" Cyrith started, almost losing her hold on Malakai who glanced back at her reassuringly.

"I...well..." Cyrith gulped. Talina turned her horse abruptly, facing them and making them pull their mount back sharply. Bretran also halted, watching everything and focusing on nothing, just as impassive as before.

Talina stared out from the depths of her hood; and despite the shadows shrouding her features, a hint of reproof marred her calm. "There is more to this than you know, girl. Do not try my patience."

Cyrith seemed to shrink in the saddle behind Malakai, but she spoke up indignantly, apparently unfazed. "Why do you get to ask all the questions? As if we were hiding something and you aren't? Elves don't ride with other kinds of men, yet you're here with him and now us. You didn't even seem surprised to see us. You go first."

Talina shot an amused glance at Bretran. "You speak the truth. Elves do not trust easily...or ride with those whose loyalties are in question." She nodded. "Yes, there is much to tell, and you, too, may have a part to play in this drama..."

She shrugged and turned her horse, starting again along the path. It was a long moment before she began to speak. "My journey began when I was barely a child. An old man spoke a prophecy over me which he said would change the world. Ever after that, I felt drawn to leave my people and wander. It began when I was barely fifty turnings. I went westward, then south. I returned to my people often in those early days. I would spend a turning at home then another traveling. As time passed, I was away for longer and longer.

"Wandering became my life. I saw the four corners of the land and even sailed out from the shores of this land

and saw another, far away. Of late, my travels have taken me to Degan."

She paused, considering, and her tone was wry when she continued. "Wandering can become a way of life, and so it was for me. I had forgotten my childhood, lost much of what tied me to my people."

She paused again, then looked back as she spoke once more. "I had forgotten, until I heard that same prophecy again, in Degan. It was as if a voice had reached up from the depths of my past and pointed the way north. Bits of that riddle had been handed down by my people, from generation to generation, ever since the Great War.

"I still do not know how it came to Degan, and I heard it purely by chance, but it awoke old memories." Talina peered through the darkness at the two children. "What do you know of Degan?"

Cyrith's tone was more relaxed now as she said, "The stories say it is the land of the Deegani—the men who hold The North against the forces of darkness."

Bretran snorted softly and Talina's gentle yet somehow bitter laugh rippled back to them. "Yes, that is what the stories say, and once it was even true. Today, the reality of the thing is a different matter. Once, the Deegani may have been men of valor and courage who stood against the darkness. Now the tale of the northlands is much more... interesting. The Deegani are warriors still, but they squabble among themselves like children while their people are slaughtered or enslaved."

Bretran grunted and this time when Talina laughed, her bitterness was plain, and she replied, as if to his grunt, "Oh, you know the truth of it."

She waved her hand in a throwaway gesture that, at the same time, indicated Bretran. "He was having... difficulties...with one of his brothers over who would succeed their father as king; so when the reports they had been receiving about bandits and raids in this area began coming from sources too reputable for his father's regency council to ignore, he came north to see for himself.

"When we arrived in Findale, we found the barracks at half muster. The men had deserted their posts, and the farmers in outlying lands have not been heard from in months. There were also strange tales passing between the villagers. We decided to continue north to find the source of the problem, despite some..." her mouth quirked, "trouble...with the captain of the guard."

Cyrith nodded, frowning. "There are only two of you?"

Talina's voice carried contempt now. "We'd no 'royal authorization' to take men from the barracks. Besides, I've my own suspicions of what has been happening here."

"And your prophecy? What has it to do with all this?"

Talina looked thoughtful, and her voice had a testing edge to it when she next spoke. "What is tonight, girl?"

Cyrith blinked, uncomprehending. "Winternight. There's only enough free magic for an easy hunt on Winternight."

Talina's shoulder twitched under her cloak. "So it is..." and her voice changed, deepening and, as she continued, ringing out through the darkness.

"On Winter's night of power,

the comrades first shall meet.

The princess of the woodlands,

the scion of watchmen bright,

The child of dwarves and fairies,

the giant from the east,

The son of fallen Simia,

the outcast from the pack,

The wizard of the shattered coast,

though present yet unseen.

Together will they forge man's fate,

together stand against the storm,

For when they find the light of yore,

shall ancient darkness wake once more."

Talina let the last words trail off into silence.

Cyrith's puzzled frown showed her incomprehension. "So the prophecy is speaking of tonight? ...but what does it mean? What darkness?"

Talina's cool, ironic smile could be heard in her voice. "If I knew, I would hardly be bumbling around the forest in the middle of the night with two children, would I?

"All I know is that that prophecy was made by one of great power—one who should be believed. ...And we may have a part to play in its fulfillment."

Cyrith nodded slowly then asked, "But why me? My people are the Fae, but I'm not even grown yet..."

Talina looked at Bretran. Voice troubled, she said, "Prophecies have been wrong before, even those kept by my people, but that prophecy comes from the Book of Yore. The Great Wizard himself wrote it, shortly after the last, terrible battle..."

They were climbing into the foothills now, and Talina was guiding her mare carefully up a slope covered with rocks and loose debris.

She fell silent for a moment choosing their path, and Cyrith asked, "The Book of Yore?"

Talina looked back at her. "Do the Fae remember nothing of the past? I speak of the greatest warrior wizard of all time, who defeated the Byzimyanny, the Nameless One, in the Battle of Ages. He left a book of prophecy behind him when he left Eschaton, and this is the first and possibly greatest of the Prophecies of Eschaton."

Suddenly the air was rent by a terrible sound—half howl, half scream—filling the night around them, echoing off the mountain ahead, and raising the hair on the backs of their necks. The packhorse and the children's mount tried to bolt, but Bretran grabbed for the halter of the children's horse and held it. The packhorse's lead rein, however, which he had held in his other hand, slipped free; and the animal went crashing off into the brush.

Bretran cursed. "Beastmen!"

4

Talina shot a disbelieving glance at Bretran, then her mouth curved into a speculative, ironic smile. "The outcast from the pack?"

Screams sounded again, three this time, and she grimaced. "And the rest of the pack, it seems." Whirling her horse Talina called, "Come!" Then she whispered something to the mare and it took off to the west at a dead run. Bretran slapped the children's horse on the rump; and, putting spurs to his own mount, followed Talina. A moment later another scream tore through the night. This one, however, came from directly ahead. Talina scarcely paused, pulling her horse back around in a tight turn, but before Bretran and the children could follow, two more screams came in rapid succession from the south and the west. Talina turned once more, this time north-east; and again they began to run, all three horses abreast. As they fairly flew toward the mountains, dodging trees, they heard another scream behind them, this time of a horse in mortal agony, cutting off as abruptly as it had begun. Then the inhuman sounds came once more, this time in a chorus that set the horses running even harder than before.

They raced on and on, each moment seeming an eternity; their horses blowing now, tiring more with every step. They were running uphill with the unnatural, black mountains looming still ahead of them, closer than ever, jutting up suddenly out of the land. All around, the trees hung motionless, and neither bird nor beast was to be seen.

The chase dragged on for what could have been minutes or hours, and through it all Talina seemed to be muttering something under her breath. Every now and then either she or Bretran would glance behind them, but mostly they fixed their gazes ahead. Again screams came from behind and to either side, and Bretran and Talina exchanged meaningful looks. They were being herded like sheep to a slaughter, and the children must have known it too judging by the glances they shot over their shoulders and the frightened way they peered ahead into the darkness. After a while they began to see patches of snow, brilliant white in the darkness, and at times they plunged through drifts of the stuff, soft and powdery.

They were under the clouds now; and soon they passed into shadow, leaving behind what little light the moon had provided. They were still running though they hadn't heard the screams for some time, and Talina was still muttering to herself.

Then, the chorus of screams came again, and a few moments later there was a crashing in the forest to their right, as if a great beast was blundering toward them through the brush. Bretran's sword cleared its sheath in an instant, and its steel glinted in what little light penetrated into the shadow of the terrible clouds. The horses were running full out, foam flecking their bodies, and still the crashing sound came closer. The trail they had been following widened suddenly, and a great shape, at least twice the height of a man, broke from the brush next to them, running parallel to their course, but less than fifty links away.

The screams sounded yet again, and the great running figure seemed to leap ahead of them along the trail, only getting closer to them as the trail began to narrow again. Then, the screams sounded again, but this time deeper and closer than ever before. Their pursuers no longer called a hunt; now they sounded the chase. Talina was still muttering to herself, but even more frantically now, and she suddenly veered off to the left into what appeared to be solid growth.

As they all came to see, it was merely a thin screen of brush, and without warning they broke from the trees into the open. Ahead of them and off to the left was a cliff that dropped sheer into darkness, doubtless, all the way to the forest below. Directly ahead lay a narrow trail along the mountain with the cliff to one side and the steep mountainside to the other.

Instead of heading along the mountain, Talina made for the brush to the right, stopping next to the mountainside just at the edge of the brush. Instantly, she was on the ground and pushing through the thicker brush that grew up along the slope. It only took a moment for her to find what she was looking for, but then she hissed and motioned Bretran forward. He swung from his horse and strode forward to where she stood. She pointed to the side of the mountain and spoke a few words. He nodded and pushed his body into the foliage, still leading his stallion.

A moment later there was muffled cursing from ahead, but as the stallion disappeared, Talina motioned for the two children to dismount and hurriedly pushed them after Bretran. She herself followed immediately behind them, leading her mare. As they pushed into the cave, they found that the entrance was just large enough for the horses to pass through, though after a few links it widened and the ceiling stretched away and upward into the darkness.

The darkness was not complete, however. A glow lay ahead and off to the left, and when they halted they could see a tiny fire against the wall. Talina pushed her horse up beside them, and, almost reflexively, the children turned to look at the mouth of the cave.

Cyrith shrieked. A huge...man?...was just getting to his feet where the cave's entrance started to widen. At eighteen or twenty links tall, he could easily have been the monstrous shape they'd seen outside. Long, wild hair and beard flowed from a face that was broad, weathered and knobbed like a great water-worn lump of volcanic rock. The eyes were massive blue and green orbs that caught the firelight and gathered it up like the eyes of a giant cat. Their colors, however, were not fixed. They changed and flowed with their gathered light, always running blue or green, with an occasional touch of yellow.

At Cyrith's scream, Talina spun and put her hand across the girl's mouth, muffling the greater part of the sound. She hissed, "By the great King himself, be silent, girl! You'll kill us all."

Cyrith raised a trembling hand and pointed at the huge figure, now standing at the entrance. Whatever she might have said was muffled by Talina's hand, but the elf responded anyway. "Yes, I know what he is. He is as caught here as we. Besides, this confirms it all."

As Cyrith blinked up at her in shock, Talina released the Fae girl and pushed past the two children toward the tiny fire where Bretran stood, his sword against the neck of what must have been the ugliest creature they had ever seen. It was short and squat, literally as wide as it was tall, with green-black skin that had odd tufts of hair poking out here and there. It wore only a breechcloth and a long-sleeved robe, open at the front, hem brushing the dirt. Its arms and legs poked out at the corners of its body almost like they had been added as afterthoughts. Its half-reptilian face was pocked and pebbled and it shone with oil in the firelight.

Talina spoke, quietly but with the same cool authority she had shown so far. "We are not safe here, but we should have a few moments. Say what you must, but by the Star, do it quietly!"

Everyone stared at her in varying mixtures of shock and befuddlement. They all stood inside the cave, firelight flickering around them, not a sound coming from any of them, except when one of the horses would stomp or snort. The raw fear of the chase still held most of them, and their minds were sluggish enough, even had there not been a great deal about their circumstances that was new to all of them.

After a moment, as if she could not sense their confusion, Talina gestured gracefully to the great shape in the entrance to the cave. "Who might you be, my lord giant?"

The figure stepped forward, away from the entrance and farther into the fire's meager light. The giant was at least twice as tall as Talina, and in the confines of the cave he had to stoop to keep his head from scraping the ceiling. He wore a loose brown cloak made of coarse wool cloth, unevenly dyed. Under the robe were trousers of the same rough weave, belted with a length of rope. In his hand, he clutched a long staff, at least as tall as he was, for he held it at an angle and it was still in danger of bringing down chunks of cave rock on their heads. It occurred to Cyrith to wonder how he had gotten it into the cave with him—or how he had gotten in himself, for that matter. He must have crawled through the entrance nearly on his belly.

The giant nodded to Talina and spoke in a voice that was deep, rumbling through the cave, even though he was obviously trying to be quiet. "Ulgoth is my name, Lady. I intended no intrusion, but I've no desire to see the beastmen any closer than I must. Their leavings are sight enough...burned farms and slaughtered livestock all the way from Grand Gorge. Only by luck have I made it so far without meeting them. I expect I would make a fair account of myself if forced, but better to avoid trouble."

Talina nodded, then turned to the hunched-over creature that Bretran still held at swordpoint. "And you?"

"I," the creature drew itself up to its full height, which was still just barely taller than Bretran's chest, "am being called Grath, and this," his hairy arms rose into a sweeping gesture, indicating the group that had crowded into his shelter, "is most rudeness." His voice was gruff, but not extraordinarily low, and it seemed too high for his bulk, especially after Ulgoth's rumble.

Grath eyed Bretran up the length of the sword, whose tip still hung a finger's width from his neck, and declaimed, "Bargering in! Pointing nasty sharp sword at Grath! Deepest shamefulness!"

Bretran snorted and raised the point of his sword a little more toward the ugly creature's chin. "Oh, and it's out of a peace loving nature you were holding that when I found you? I don't fancy a troll lovetap." He pointed with his chin at a huge, gnarled hunk of wood that looked to be a club of some sort, a few links away on the floor.

Grath brought his hands up in a half-shrug of protest. "Must have protection. Half-men want to eat Grath. Been trying for days and days."

Talina raised a hand and said to Bretran, "Peace, son of Degran, there is no harm for us in this one, I think. Troll he may be, but he is hardly a beast, less still a were-man, and besides..." She trailed off with a slight twitch of her shoulders.

Bretran's lips flattened in a half-irritated, half-ironic line and he lowered the sword until the point rested against his boot. For a moment, he seemed about to speak, then his taciturn nature reasserted itself and he subsided. Grath sniffed at Bretran, then began straightening and patting at the loose robe he wore.

5

Talina looked around and nodded. "Shall we move deeper? We dare not attract the wrong sort of attention by lingering here."

She started to take a step forward, but Cyrith planted her hands on her hips and said challengingly, "You mean we're just letting them come with us?"

Talina frowned at her, obviously irritated, and asked, "You remember the prophecy, girl:

The princess of the woodlands,

the scion of watchmen bright,

The child of dwarves and fairies,

the giant from the east,

The son of fallen Simia..." Talina nodded to each of their party as she recited.

Cyrith frowned and motioned to her companion. "And what of Malakai? I hear nothing of him in those prophecies."

Talina flicked her head from side to side. "You ask for answers I do not possess. I am neither scholar nor seer."

Cyrith sniffed loudly. "In that case, how did you find this cave? And how did he follow us," she indicated Ulgoth, who stood impassively behind them. "if the... werethings ... can't?" Cyrith gave an involuntary glance toward the entrance to their cave.

Talina's mouth curved into a half-amused expression. "As to that, elf magic is strong with the trees and living things. Confusing our scents was a bit difficult, but it should lead them a merry chase. ...and," she frowned. "This place has a peculiar feel to it. It...called...to me. Even had I not been able to find it by other means, its presence would have impressed itself on me."

Talina shook her head and pointed deeper into the cave. "And now, we had best move on. If you two will accompany us, we can talk more... wherever this leads." She cocked an eyebrow at Grath. "Have you explored the cave to any depth? We'd best get inward and away from the were-men. There is still a smell of us coming from this place."

Grath's face contorted into a grimace. "Goes deep deep. Smell magic." He shrugged. "No like magic." Then his face contorted more and he bared his teeth. "No like magic; hate half-men. I come."

Talina nodded and seemed about to speak, but Ulgoth cleared his throat and shook his head. "Pardon me, lady, I know nothing of prophecies, but even so, I, too, may accompany you. I've no love for the... were-men you called them?"

The giant's voice rumbled from deep in his chest, and he fixed his eyes on Talina. "I will ask, however. To whom do you give your allegiance? Mine belongs to the King of Yore. I keep no company with his enemies."

There was silence for a moment then Bretran grunted and said drily, "Allegiance is a touchy question on this side of the ocean, giant." Bretran's observation was, if anything, an understatement.

The Great Oath magically bound those who spoke it to follow the one to whom they pledged. In the previous age, the Oath had been given only to great powers, such as the King of Yore or his enemy, the Nameless One. In the modern day, it was a much chancier business, and knowing another's allegiance could give one power over them, binding as the Oath was.

Ulgoth stared at him levelly, immovable and suddenly incredibly dangerous. "Allegiance is a touchy question the world over, Deegani, yet these are extraordinary circumstances. I walk not with the enemies of the King." Then he frowned, "Your people are said to serve, Deegani. You should hardly fear to answer...unless it is not so."

Grath shrugged his massive shoulders. "Grath serves King. Not afraid." He shuffled his feet awkwardly, then looked challengingly at the rest of the party, daring any of them to criticize his bold declaration.

Bretran, too, shrugged. "My people serve more in word than deed, but I've naught to lose by answering. My sword is the King's."

Cyrith sniffed. "There is no master worthy of allegiance among the Folk. The Fae serve others with many words, and only themselves in truth. The Oath is held quiet among us... For me, I serve the King." Malakai smiled a half amused, half ironic smile and nodded agreement.

Talina raised an eyebrow, then gave an ironic half smile herself. "My people hold to the old ways. I, too, serve the King."

Ulgoth shook his head, sadly. "Among the giants, there are few who claim the King as master in this age, and fewer still who serve with their hearts as well as their tongues, much less swear to his service. Yet of those I am one.

"My path, then, lies with you." He glanced down the tunnel. "...And we are all King's men. We've naught to fear."

Talina frowned. "Come then." She stepped forward, leading her mare deeper into the mountain. The children followed, walking side by side leading their horse. Leading his stallion, Bretran made a point of following Grath to keep an eye on him. Ulgoth brought up the rear.

As they continued, the cave grew dimmer and dimmer, but in the little light they had, the party could see that the walls had opened out somewhat more, and Ulgoth no longer had to stoop to avoid the ceiling. There was a decidedly musty smell to the air, and the floor and walls were smooth and grew more perfectly so with every step.

After a minute or two, Talina half turned and said, "I think it is no accident we found this place, and this tunnel was not made by natural means." Soon the darkness around them was complete. Talina walked more and more slowly until the group was just inching along, feeling their way forward like worms in the darkness. They continued that way for what seemed like hours, the rustle of their movement loud in their ears, their footfalls echoing from the polished walls.

Grath was grumbling quietly, monotonously, his epithets punctuated by the thump... thump... thump of Ulgoth's staff, when a light appeared in the middle of the group, half-blinding them all. Bretran's sword came out, and Talina whipped around; but the light dimmed to a bearable level so they could see a tiny ball of blue flame hovering over Cyrith's hand. She looked at their startled expressions and blinked in surprise.

"Sorry. There's a ley line down there." She pointed at the floor. "I just felt it. It must be coming to the surface."

Bretran sheathed his sword, uttering a soft oath as Talina nodded and Ulgoth rumbled, "Or mayhap we go down to meet it. Seems rather a large one. For one so young, you've skill if you're able to tap that." Grath made a harsh sound of disgust and they resumed their slow, trudging walk downward into the bowels of the mountain.

With Cyrith's light as a guide, they proceeded at a more reasonable rate, but whether they traveled for an hour or a day none of them could afterward have said. It was a long time, certainly, and they all fell into a semi-stupor, pressing ahead, step-by-step, through the darkness. Talina wondered, as she walked, why time was so strange. It might have been a week since the night began, yet she had no doubt it was barely midnight. They walked for what might have been an age, and time crawled past at a trickle. She wondered, but had no answer.

Slowly, as they moved deeper into the mountain, the stone turned from the gray it had been near the entrance to a deep, light-consuming black that seemed to drain away the tiny ball still flickering over Cyrith's outstretched hand. It was some time before Talina noticed, and the nagging doubts she had felt since entering the cave flared up inside her. Something about what lay ahead seemed wrong, just as had the wind in the clearing; something beyond sensing but there all the same. There was something about the earth itself that was evil in a way she couldn't quite define. Still she kept on. There was no going back—not with were-men outside...

The trek was a long one, and their minds, already weary from the long chase, were lulled into a stupor by the monotony of putting one foot in front of another, and the darkness of the deep earth. Time took on an ephemeral quality, elastic and not easy to recognize. Reality became a repetition of step, step, step, one after another until their minds were numbed and dull.

It was barely noticeable at first, something that nagged at minds befuddled by the darkness; but didn't quite bring itself to their notice. Slowly, imperceptibly, the light in the tunnel had been increasing. After a time, it easily outshone Cyrith's little flame. The walls were still the same unblemished, black stone, but light seeped through it to fill the tunnel with a strange radiance. The process was so gradual that Talina didn't even notice until she stepped directly out into the full glare of a blazing, white light.

It was like being thrust suddenly onto a stage before an audience of thousands. Talina felt more exposed than she ever had in her life. She stopped stock still and slowly backed up until she was again hidden in the shadows. The sudden stop had alerted the others, and Malakai and Cyrith crowded up beside Talina, with Bretran and Grath on her other side, now staring ahead out of the passage. Ulgoth's height allowed him to watch over the rest of the party's heads. Talina followed their gaze, and what she saw caught her eye and held it.

6

Ahead—well over a hundred links ahead—was a pool of light that reflected itself off the smooth, midnight-black stone. The light was dim at the edges, so there was no obvious line where the light stopped and the darkness began. At the center, however, the circle of stone was as well-lit as a summer's day. What was really odd about the sight was that the stone was still entirely black, and the light seemed to reflect from it only by virtue of their total incompatibility.

Cyrith stirred and yawned then stopped still at the sight. Slowly, Talina led them forward and out into the light, looking warily around. The light, they saw as they filed hesitantly out of the passage, came from a brilliant point that hung in mid air, far, far above them.

They slowly walked toward the pool of brilliance, leading the horses and gazing up at the light's source. Strangely, the light did not blind them, but neither could they see what actually caused it. The glow was fierce but cold, and they stared at it, mesmerized.

The group stopped, as if by one accord, as they approached the place where the light began to reflect from the stone at their feet. For long moments, they simply stood, their eyes fixed on the brilliance above them.

"Beautiful, isn't it?" They all looked down from their reverie to see Malakai seated cross-legged on the floor, just where the light began to brighten.

All of them, even Talina, blinked at him in incomprehension, and he smiled whimsically, almost ironically. "The light has shone on this floor for nearly two thousand turnings." He shook his head, eyes distant. "Back then, it was so bright it lit the cavern like daylight. On Winternight, the mountains glowed with it. The power is fading, the binding growing weaker." Malakai broke off for a moment, then, in the still-stupefied silence he asked, "Would you like to see?"

Cyrith nodded, awe painted across her face. "Please?"

Malakai smiled and said, "A moment, then, little sister." He got to his feet and turned away from them to gaze upward. After a moment, in total silence, the light began to descend.

By this time, the group's consternation had turned to questions. Every single one of the party was near to bursting with them. Still, none broke the silence, and Malakai continued to stare up at the growing light for a long time as it slowly descended until it hovered barely twice Ulgoth's height above them, shining ever more brightly in the darkness. They could see, now, that the light emanated from a crystal the size of two fists held together and filled with blue-white radiance.

"You are fortunate." Malakai said, slowly turning back to them. "But perhaps...not as most would measure it." He looked bemused for a moment, as if having some inner conversation none of them could hear, then he shook his head.

"Do you know why you are here?" He looked at each of them in turn—a long, hard look as if searching for something, then he turned and began to pace slowly back and forth.

None of them answered. The sheer presence Malakai exerted made it obvious that he wasn't simply a little boy. "You are here to fulfill your oath. Master Ulgoth came closer than he knew when he asked our allegiance." Malakai paused, smiling a bit ironically. "Each of you swore fealty to one this world has all but forgotten." His eyes swept over them again. "Many pay him lip service, but few remember there is a living man behind the name...or if they do, they do not believe he will ever return to claim his due. Even you, who have bound yourselves to him with the Great Oath only know him as an idea. He is at best a distant reality to you, an absent ideal.

"Few indeed have bound themselves to him with the Oath. To most of the world, the King of Yore is nothing more than an old story. The Sidhe are a mere ghost of a memory; a legend, perhaps. Even you, though you believe enough to pledge him your life, know very little of his reality—or of what that oath meant.

"The world is about to change, my friends. I would say that your faithfulness is to be rewarded, but in the short term, that reward will be trials more severe than you can imagine...but the battle that comes upon us is the most important in the history of Eschaton.

"The final battle is beginning, and the faithful of the King must be prepared for it. That is why you have been gathered here this Winternight."

Malakai turned fully toward them and said, with a ghost of a smile, "Our time is limited. I'm sure you have questions. I will answer as I may, but I have no time or patience for foolishness."

Talina's was the first voice to break the silence. "Who are you, boy...or what are you, really?"

Malakai's mouth quirked. "I told you. My name is Malakai. ...As to WHAT—well, there is a more interesting question." He considered a moment. "I have been many things—a traveler, a warrior, a diplomat, and a prince. Of late, I have been a brother to one in need. To you, I am a messenger. But first and always, I am a liegeman of the King." With that, he bowed his head for a moment, then stared straight at Talina. Gaze intense, he asked, "And what are you, Lady? ...You are a princess among your people, but you have run away from your responsibilities to chase a fancy."

Talina looked aghast. "I have sought to fulfill the prophecies of Yore!"

Malakai shook his head. "Honesty will serve you better."

Talina shrank back and seemed about to bolt. "Grandfather—In'Kalith himself said I would never be an elder! What do you ask of me?"

Malakai's voice was gentle. "You are asked only to fulfill the promise you made to His Majesty so many turnings ago. Do you remember?" Talina nodded timidly, her usual self-assurance reduced to confusion.

Malakai looked at each of them in turn. "Do not mistake me. You were called here, each in your own way. You have done well to come."

He fell silent for a moment, and Bretran pointed at the crystal. "To be in command of such a wonder, you must be a great wizard. Why did you not save us, even the one you claim as sister, from the were-men?"

Malakai shook his head. "I am no wizard, or not as you might think of such things," he said thoughtfully. "And even had I the power to do as you say, what gain would we have from it? The first lesson a great wizard must learn is that greatness is found far more in using well what you have been given than in the magnitude of your power. The smallest pebble can dam the mightiest river, if it falls into place properly." He shook his head again, emphatically. "No. Had I interfered it would have called worse onto our heads than a few Changers."

Then Malakai cocked his head. "But what of your friends, and those you call your people? True, you are no wizard, but you have influence enough. Haven't you the power to save the freeholders if you choose?"

Bretran shrugged. "I am no king. The council decides. If I usurp them now, I will inherit nothing."

Malakai sneered. "You put your own pride before your subjects' lives. What sort of king would you be?"

Bretran countered, his face stormy, "In war, a commander must not lose his command for fear of casualties. Nor am I responsible for the freeholders. They're not sworn to the crown."

Malakai's face fell. "So says one reclaimed at great cost from the greatest enemy of all...and what of The Sword? How many must pay for your pride?"

Bretran paled and bowed his head, and Malakai turned to Cyrith with a smile. "I see you waiting, little sister. What say?"

Cyrith's eyes widened. "This means you're leaving…" She stared at him hard, trying not to cry. "…doesn't it?" Her eyes started to tear up. "Don't you care for me?"

Malakai's smile was bittersweet. "Dear little sister, you knew it must happen someday. Will you wound me for a departure whose time has come?"

Cyrith hung her head as silent tears began to drip from her face. "Sorry. I… I…"

Malakai's smile turned gentle. "Yes, dear one. I love you, too. Remember what was promised. Eyes clear." She nodded, head still bowed, then asked, "You've told me much of the King. But…what is he? Is he a man? One of the gods?"

Malakai's twisted smile reappeared. "What is a man? Is a man a Sidhe? a Gygan? one of the Fae, perhaps? …and what of the gods? Are the Dragons gods? The youngest dragon spawned before the first Sidhe walked the face of Eschaton, yet even they die when their purpose ends. What of the Engyls? A great Engyl could stir the Cauldron like a bowl of soup, yet they are feared as demons if men know of them at all. …and there are men who worship rocks. What makes a god?

"As to the King, he is as much a man as you or I—or perhaps," Malakai's mouth quirked. "Better to say that we are as human as he is. There has never been a man to equal him, nor has any other man walking the face of Eschaton lived since before the Betrayal.

"Your question has no easy answer. He is what he is."

Cyrith nodded thoughtfully and Malakai smiled at her. "I daren't carry on too long, little sister. We have yet to complete our purpose here." He raised an eyebrow at Ulgoth. "What of you?"

Ulgoth shuffled his great feet, and cleared his throat uneasily, the unselfconscious stolidity he had shown so far now absent. "What question dare I ask, young master, when I know that I, too, have much to be ashamed of?"

Malakai looked at the giant speculatively. "So cleverness leads you to refuse? Or is it pride that seeks to hide your shortcomings? Fear perhaps?"

Ulgoth looked thoughtful, then shook his head ruefully. "Say what you will then, young master. I stand at your pleasure. You need not await any question of mine to make your condemnation."

Malakai shook his head. "Do not misunderstand. I do not speak to condemn you. The path ahead is steep. You cannot afford pride or fear. They will undo you."

Malakai turned to Grath and nodded. "And you?"

Grath brought one ham-size hand up to his chin and squeezed thoughtfully. "Why Grath here?"

Malakai raised his eyebrows. "You're asking me why you came?"

Grath shook his head vehemently. "No, no, no. Grath told to come. Grath come. What do now?"

Malakai smiled. "Listen. Watch. Learn. Make new friends. Then go home and take care of your family. They will need you in the time to come."

Grath nodded, satisfied, and Malakai's gaze swept across the rest of the little party as if seeking something. He waited a moment, then nodded and bowed his head.

7

There was silence as Malakai began pacing back and forth through the edge of the light. The little party of travelers simply stood, watching. Suddenly, Malakai stopped and looked at them, and behind him something began to take shape in the light coming down from the crystal. Patterns of light coalesced in mid air, colors seeping from white lines to form a great landscape in the air before them.

Then, as they watched, the landscape morphed and changed—once, twice, three times, then again and again, faster and faster, finally blurring out into a field of shifting luminescence.

"This is our world," Malakai said, as the scene finally came to rest, a perfect representation of the black mountains under which they stood. "The world is a brutal place." As Malakai spoke, the scene changed to a huge beast, tearing at something on the ground. Its head came up and a man's foot could be seen protruding from its mouth. Cyrith gasped in horror, and turned her face away as the beast gulped down the leg, then rapidly morphed and changed, leaving what might have been a man in its place, if it wasn't twisted and misshapen.

"The seven races are at each others' throats. Life—even the life of men—is worth little. There have been generations of war between the Changers and the Deegani. Their hatred for one-another is implacable. No quarter is given to civilians on either side, even women or children.

"Open war may yet be avoided among many of the races, but conflict is everywhere. Mistrust and treachery are more the rule than the exception.

"The Theurgans hold the Simianites in their thrall. But for a few scattered tribes, the entire race of Simia is enslaved by its more magical brothers. Nor is slaving practiced only by the Theurgans. The Changers and the Fae often keep their brothers in bondage, and there are those who hold slaves among all the races."

The scene changed again, this time to a group of men, as grotesque as the first, gathered beneath a great rock, upon which another man, tattooed all over and holding bones in either hand, stood shaking his fists above his head. Then, he raised face and hands to the sky in supplication. At his feet, another knelt, obviously of the same race as he, but bound, with his head bowed. The tattooed one replaced the bones in his belt and brought out a knife, then raised it above his head and plunged it into his victim. Once, twice, a third time. The bound form before him slumped as the tattooed figure again raised its hands to the sky, howling its triumph.

Malakai's voice was raw with anger and his eyes flashed. "This one claims to be a direct representative of His Majesty, yet he treats his own people as slaves. Those who disobey are executed as blood sacrifices. Their life force is siphoned off to feed the shamans' magic. Abuse of the king's authority is as vile as it is widespread."

The scene changed to show a group of giants, gathered in a circle around a stone altar. One giant held a deer, its legs bound together, head tucked safely under one of his great arms. Another giant held a huge knife with which he gently, almost tenderly, cut into the deer's neck.

Malakai shook his head. "Blood-sacrifice, too, is everywhere, though the people cloak it in pretty euphemisms and petty excuses."

The light behind Malakai shifted to a bright haze and he said, his voice heavy, "It has not always been so. Once the world was a brighter place—before the Cataclysm and the Great War.

"Then, the world was home to the Sidhe, the men of old. They were bound to the world by their magic, and all the creatures of the earth were their subjects. In those days, the King himself walked Eschaton. It was long ago, and much of what we remember is half-truths and tales grown large in the retelling.

"It was in the Cataclysm that the world of today was born—out of fire and chaos and destruction. When the land and its magic were sundered, so were the people of the land, and the seven races of man are all that remain of the great Sidhe."

Malakai trailed off with a frown and considered for a moment before continuing. "There are many tales of the Cataclysm. Some believe it was the work of the Nameless One and his followers—that he sundered the world out of spite and hatred, jealous of the King's favor, and the King left in sorrow for the land from which he came in time beyond memory. Others hold that the cataclysm was the result of a great war, that the King and the Nameless One rent the world with their battle, that the Nameless One was destroyed and the King was driven away by the terrible magics they released. Some say the King himself was responsible—that he was displeased with the Sidhe in their pride, and set the Nameless One upon them, to tear the world asunder and enslave all who survived.

"There are many more tales—vile ones, foolish ones, and some very, very dangerous ones."

Malakai shrugged and began to pace again. "It is not my affair which of the tales you believe. If your heart would know the truth then in time you will find it." His lips twisted into a wry grin. "Very little of it bears on what I must tell you. You need only know that your forefathers left you a legacy of chains that remains to this day.

"Just as the Sidhe were bound to the land, so they could bind themselves, at will, to whatever or whoever they chose. The Old Magic was stronger and more enduring than the very bedrock of the world. Bits remain, even today."

He paused for a moment and smiled wryly. "Among the Sidhe, allegiance was a matter of pride, not shame or fear as it is now. Ille' Breela Ee'Hoenye, the Great Oath, is one such remnant of Old Magic, though it has but a shadow of the power."

There was a hiss of indrawn breath from one or two of the little party and Bretran snorted. "The Oath is unbreakable. What can be more powerful?"

Malakai's smile went crooked. "Not unbreakable. Infernally difficult to break. Powerful and dangerous, but not unbreakable. ...The Old Magic was... well... a step beyond even unbreakable, for it is the Old Magic itself that holds the world together. It is Old Magic that makes the sun rise and fall, and Old Magic that holds the moon in its place. It is impossible even to imagine breaking the old magic, for it defines existence."

It was as if Bretran's question had broken a barrier of some sort, and Cyrith piped up, "What do you mean?"

Malakai stopped pacing, and his face was deadly serious. "I mean that you are still bound by the greatest oath ever sworn—an oath your ancestors swore to the Nameless One itself. You are not bound as they were. Even the Old Magic wanes with the generations, but bound more closely than if you spoke the Great Oath to the Nameless One right now, even if not as tightly."

"You speak in riddles, young master." Ulgoth shook his head. "I hear your words without understanding. You speak wonders, but what do they mean?"

Malakai shrugged. "Simply that much of the world still serves the Nameless One, whatever they may think or will."

Bretran snorted again. "I don't believe in fate."

Malakai looked at him with an irritated frown. "Nor I, but this is not fate, and it is no less true. Allegiance is held both sacred and secret today, and for good reason. What happens when a liege man tries to break the Great Oath?"

Bretran blinked. "He cannot. His own mind will rebel unto death. He is compelled."

Malakai nodded. "Just so. ...But," he gave a twisted smile, "even bindings in the Old Magic can be broken, given time, and the King will remember his own, though the rest of the world may forget him.

"There are a few, like us, who have sworn themselves to the King, and for us, the fetters of Abomination are broken."

Ulgoth shook his great head, almost in disbelief. "To half the world, even among those who claim to believe, the

King is a myth, yet you speak as if you know him. Two-thirds of the world has forgotten the Gan-Anim, the nameless, yet you say they are bound to his service. If it is so, how could so few know of it?"

Malakai nodded at Ulgoth's question then looked around at the others. "Bear with me a little longer. It will become clear."

He resumed pacing, then continued, "As little as we remember of the Cataclysm, we know what followed in terrible detail. Eschaton settled in an age of confusion and chaos, then a time of peace—or so it seemed. The Nameless One built a kingdom that enslaved half of Eschaton, and would have enslaved the rest, but for the Wizard."

The air behind Malakai, which had remained empty for a long time, again began to shimmer and take on form. When the light had gathered, it showed a forest, malformed and grotesque. The trees were alive, but would never be healthy, and there was no beauty left in them. Everything about the scene was warped, and the plants looked poisonous.

"There was nothing he did not twist to his purposes." The scene changed to show a great black shape, like a bear but bigger and bulkier. It was tearing at something unrecognizable and mutilated that struggled to escape, but could not. "The plants, the animals, the birds... Everything became his tool. The men were the worst. By far."

Malakai shuddered and looked hard at each of them as the light behind him rippled, then finally disappeared like smoke. "I will not show you what he can do to a human if we choose to allow it. You will learn soon enough."

Malakai subsided again and looked thoughtful. "Now as to the Wizard... Some say he was one of the Sidhe, come back to fight for the world he loved. Some say it was the King himself, returned to do battle with his ancient foe. Some say it was the King's son, or his servant, or another of his people. Some believe there was no Wizard—that one of the great princes of Degan joined the Giants to do battle with the Nameless One.

"Most say the Wizard went to battle with the Nameless One and destroyed it, then returned from this world to the one from where he came. The little we know of him comes from the Book of Yore, the prophecies he left behind. Many have puzzled over the book and found little of use.

"Today, men say there was no wizard, or even that there was no Nameless One. After the great war, they disappeared. It has been thousands of turnings since the Battle of Ages. Most have forgotten. It is easy to doubt, with the Wizard gone and the Nameless One with him.

"Most would rather doubt than know, for it allows them to do as they will. Their lives are easier when they forget. The Nameless One has become a story to scare the children. Only a few remember at all, and they are more often the Nameless One's own followers."

"Time turns and the world moves on. All is forgotten."

Malakai nodded to Ulgoth. "There is your explanation, big brother, though there is more, even than that."

The light behind Malakai rippled yet again, and he said, half to himself, "So much forgotten. So much lost..."

8

Then, turning his attention fully back to them, he smiled at Bretran. "You called me a wizard. What you call magic is... well, first it is energy—power that can be manipulated by those with the gift and the knowledge. Raw energy can be turned to many purposes— more easily destruction than life.

"The Nameless One was not always a creature of flesh and blood. First it was an Engyl, a being made wholly of magic. The Engyls are creatures unlike us. They do not even live in our world. We do not know where they come from or how they were made.

"But the Nameless One was not content to be as it was. By a great working, one more powerful than any other ever attempted, it was made flesh, and became the greatest enemy to this world that has ever been. You see, by the King's decree only men can rule this world, and control is what the Nameless craves."

Malakai paused and his lip curled in something between disgust and bitterness. "The Watchmen call him Nameless. You," Malakai looked at Talina. "You call him Byzimyanny." He turned his gaze to Ulgoth. "You say Gan-Anym. To the Fae he is Ynaithnid, to the Simianites

Degahyaso. The Theurgans know him as Nyvtelen; the Changers as Ynami. All mean the same. To this world, he is the Nameless One. None call him by his rightful name for fear they may call his attention down upon them. For his followers, it is a token of respect."

Malakai frowned. "Many are right to fear. We who are sworn to the King need not. His rightful name is Sheklah, Disturber of All. Sheklah, the Defiler. Sheklah, the Never-man." There were sounds of distress from one or two of them, and Malakai smiled a bit ruefully before continuing, "The world from which Sheklah came, the world of magic, is ethereal, ever-changing and shaped to the will of any creature that lives there—or here. This world is dust and stone, unyielding and solid. Sheklah's will is to change the world to fit its own perverse whim. The weak are its slaves; the strong are its enemies. It sees no other way." Malakai paused to look at each of them seriously. "...And it is coming back."

Again, Malakai stared hard at each of them. "So you learn what your service is to be. The end of the age approaches. I tell you now—Sheklah was not destroyed. It was only defeated..."

"And locked away here!" Cyrith interrupted, excitedly. The other members of the party stared at her, as if she'd interrupted some sort of solemn, religious ceremony. Perhaps in a way, she had, but Malakai only smiled at her quizzically.

"Locked away? Why do you say so, little sister?"

"Because... that's the rhyme. 'Locked away, An age to stay, Asleep and entombed in the black land's womb,'" Cyrith proclaimed.

Malakai opened his mouth as if to speak, then visibly rethought what he'd been about to say. He shrugged. "As you say, its power was broken and bound, sealed away from the world."

He stared at the floor beneath their feet. "Of Sheklah itself, only the Wizard knows ...but his seal weakens a bit more every day, sapped and eaten away by the darkness of this place." He pointed to the great crystal, shining down upon them.

"...And Sheklah knows. Such is its nature, to yearn and hate and strain for the destruction of any who might not submit to its tortured will. There are still those who follow it—a few by consent and consciously, and many by pride and fear and hate, tied to it by an ancient promise that may not be broken.

"It is to Sheklah's advantage that the people do not believe, so that when it comes once more into its full power, the world is unprepared for it and unbelieving." He smiled a wry, twisted smile. "The ones who scoff loudest are often its own followers, for the first and most potent of the enemy's weapons is a lie, and that," Malakai paused and looked at each of them meaningfully, "is how you will know it and its ilk. Where truth is, hope is."

Talina looked thoughtfully at Malakai and said, "It has been many an age since the Byzimyanny's..." She stopped and looked at Malakai with an eyebrow raised. "...since Sheklah's defeat, but the elves still remember. The world was a terrible place, ravaged and torn. It is said that the very rocks cried out in agony at the corruption." Her eyes were far away, as if remembering something, then she cocked her head slightly. "What would you have us do?"

Malakai nodded to her, appreciative. "Return home, lady. Return home and prepare. There were to be seven of you. I see five." His eyes glinted and he searched each face carefully. "Five of you to carry the most important news this world has ever heard. Five of you to prepare the way. The Wizard, too, will return when the time is right, and that is what you must tell them."

Then, in an instant, Malakai's eyes turned hard as steel and bright as the noon-day sun, and his voice rang through the cavern, sending back echoes from walls impossibly distant. "There is no middle ground. Tell them that the time of the Reckoning is coming."

Malakai bowed his head and when he looked up again, his voice was calm and gentle. "I have told you that we stand upon the tomb of the greatest evil in the history of Eschaton. Have you not wondered that none of Sheklah's allies wait here to guard it?"

He looked at Bretran. "You asked why I did not intervene. This place is one of the most dangerous in the world. It is guarded, on one hand, by the greatest talisman of the greatest Wizard the world has ever known, by traps, magical and mechanical, by a maze of tunnels and passageways that honeycombs the entire mountain range, and by secrets even I do not know. On the other hand are the closest and most powerful allies of evil incarnate, as well as the lowest rabble of the underworld, attracted by the pull of its magic.

"This is all that keeps them at bay...the worst of them." Malakai pointed up at the light above their heads.

"Look." Malakai pointed outward, away from the light, and as their eyes followed his hand, the great crystal flashed, its light so bright it should have blinded them.

Standing on three sides of their little pool of light, just out of reach in what had been the darkness, were creatures from a nightmare. All three were the same, with a shape to haunt the darkest of dreams. The flash of blue-white light seemed to absorb into flesh as black as the walls themselves; the darkness of their forms spreading into great wings that reached out, and out, and out from them to fill the air above the little party. The creatures' shape was surprisingly well-defined even in the dimness, but it was the dull, blood-red eyes that brought true horror. Whatever they had once been, pure torment had shaped their current form, and the distilled evil they embodied pulled at the little party's minds. They seemed to reach into the very soul and bring out the darkest fears and hatreds to feed upon them.

Then, the light had faded. They all stood there in shock, Malakai simply frowning, the rest huddling closer to the center of their circle of light—light that they now realized was life itself to the little party.

"Dark Engyls?" Cyrith's voice was hardly above a whisper, and her eyes were wide as twin moons.

Malakai smiled sadly. "Engyls once, perhaps. Not now. Engyls are free creatures, temperamental, but not evil. These...these are daemons, engyls bound to Sheklah's will and forced to serve it against their own purpose.

"Sheklah's first aim is to break the spirit, and the engyls are spirit in its truest form—magic. These have been broken and remade so many times they are now mere reflections of their master's will."

He smiled humorlessly. "Gargyls are worse, and there are others, but most have not been seen since the Great

War. They chose Sheklah of their own free will. Those that remain hide, now, awaiting its return."

"How did we not meet those before?" Bretran's mouth quirked. "I'm not ungrateful... I'd fight a whole tribe of were-men before one of them."

Malakai just shrugged. "It is Winternight. Time, distance...even reality itself runs strangely here. Especially on Winternight. And," his mouth quirked. "You had special protection. You came unknowing, bearing no thought of Sheklah... and you all bear the mark of the King.

"But that does not guarantee your way out—or even your passage beyond our three... hosts. Steel is no impediment to such as them. That much, however, I may be able to help you with. After that, well, your best option is speed."

"It's a node, isn't it?" Cyrith asked, cutting Malakai off. He blinked in confused surprise, then chuckled. "Yes, there is a ley node not far away...and that tunnel follows a major ley line."

Cyrith frowned. "Major ley lines are so... so big. That little bit of fire was hard. I don't know how much I can draw without losing control."

Malakai nodded. "That ley line was one of the reasons we got in so easily. Even creatures sensitive to magic find it difficult to see those who walk so close to the big ley lines. No fear, little sister. You need not risk it. I can do you one last service."

Abruptly, he turned to Bretran. "Take care of her, watchman." He motioned to Cyrith, then turned and pointed back the way they came. "It is time for you to go."

⛰

9

Cyrith opened her mouth to argue, but Malakai said, "The night is waning. Soon the light from the crystal will fade. You do not want to be here then."

Talina nodded abruptly and motioned to the others and suddenly they were moving. Talina had swung up on her mare, and Bretran pulled Cyrith up in front of him. Bretran held the lead rein for the third horse, which Grath had somehow clambered onto. The beast didn't look too happy, but as Bretran and Talina turned to go, it bolted after the other two, directly for the cave where they had entered.

Before they were clear of the circle of light, the great crystal flared and white light shone on the midnight-black cavern wall around the entrance, reflecting from it in the same eerie way as on the floor earlier. Now, however, the radiance was mixed with a painful red light that seemed to sear into the rock.

As they passed from sight, something compelled each of them to glance back. Malakai still stood directly under the crystal, while facing him from three directions, the daemons stood upon the jet black rock of the cave floor.

Voice strong and clear, Malakai called, "Be gone from this place! Your time is not yet come! A prison awaits you! Go!" The sight lasted for a seemingly interminable moment...then, they were inside the cave, bending low over their horses' necks, dodging blindly around corners none of the riders could see. The horses seemed to know their way however and there was something about the cavern they had just left that urged both horses and riders onward, not allowing them to think of what might lie ahead.

It was the nameless terror of something impossible yet real—come to life in some horrible insanity. Only Cyrith tore free for long enough to cry, "Malakai! Maalaakaaaii!"

They were dodging through the passageway only a few moments away from the cavern when light pierced through the darkness of the mountain, washing away the black of the stone and turning the rock a glowing, pulsing white. It lasted for a mere moment before the black stone absorbed the light as if it had never been. Then the sound hit; a roar of rage and combat and destruction like some terrible force of nature frustrated in the act of tearing its enemy to pieces. The sound passed as quickly as the light, and silence reigned once more. The silence was somehow even more terrible though, and the horses raced on, hooves noiseless against the black stone.

They ran for a long time, the horses' breath heavy in the enclosed space, the terror never fading even with the time it took to run the length of the cave. It was a time immeasurable in the darkness, before they broke out, seemingly all at once into the same night they had left behind...how long had it been? The same night? It seemed impossible.

They reined up, and Bretran stared back into the cave as Ulgoth crawled out of it on hands and knees, nearly scraping his back on the low arch at the exit. Talina, however, moved farther out from the cliff, glancing around uneasily. Their exit from the cave had brought them back to their senses, and the terror of their long run was fading. As her senses cleared, however, Talina's uneasiness shifted in another direction. There was something wrong...

None of them saw the figures step out of the surrounding woods. It was as if they were a part of the forest itself until one spoke. Then, somehow they were all just there, as if they'd been there the entire time. "Ahhhh, you have returned. The Dark Lord said you would, but I scarcely believed." The voice had a hissing, rasping quality; and Talina started violently, wheeling her horse to face the speaker who laughed loudly in amusement.

"You didn't think I saw you when you did your little disappearing trick? We know better than to go into that place." He eyed the cave balefully.

"You are one of the Changers? What pack do you claim?"

The creature's eyes flashed. "You have no right to use that name!" Then he smiled. "...and I serve the Dark Lord, none other." The Were-Man sounded lazy, like a cat toying with its food. "However, when the aims of the pack match the aims of the Dark Lord, I will not complain." The Were-Men had left a slight gap on the cliff side of their formation when they had stepped from the trees and Talina found herself edging toward it along with the others as their enemies slowly closed in. There were at least a dozen of them, probably fifteen.

As they drew nearer, Talina eyed the cliff at her back. More fun to corner your prey before you kill it, she thought grimly; maybe even push it off a cliff, which is what was going to happen if they kept advancing.

The Were-Man seemed amused. "You did lead us a merry chase you know..." Suddenly Bretran lunged at one side of the formation, pulling back on his reins, his horse rearing, hooves flailing. At the same time he pulled out his sword and swung it around, catching one of the Were-Men across the head. His stallion had picked its own target, and a forehoof came crashing down on another of the creatures. It screamed and fell backward to lie writhing in the snow, clutching its face as yellow blood streamed between its fingers. The exposed parts of its body immediately began to change, twisting and growing until it was more beast than man. On the other side of Bretran, the same thing was happening to the other creature. Seeing the gap Bretran had made, Talina spoke to her horse, which plunged through to the other side of the enemy line. Meanwhile, Grath had taken a flying leap from the pack horse to land on another of the Were-Men and twist its head around in a full circle with his unbelievable Simianite strength. He immediately proceeded to leap on yet another and wrestle it toward the ground. As Talina watched, Grath took hold of one of his enemy's shoulders and wrenched its arm impossibly far backward. It howled in anguish and disbelief as the limb dropped useless to its side.

Ulgoth was keeping a full five of the creatures busy with his huge staff: striking at one, then blocking another. They simply didn't have the reach to attack him effectively without falling to his staff. That left too many, however, and they were rushing forward. Bretran spurred his horse, trying to pull through; but at precisely the wrong moment a changer jumped on the pack horse and it reared screaming into the air. Bretran was still holding its lead; and he was pulled from his saddle, his horse bolting forward with Cyrith somehow still on its back.

Bretran quickly regained his feet, but there were simply too many of the enemy. The only way to live was to give ground. A creature on the left struck out just too far, overbalancing itself; and Bretran too struck, ducking the creature's blow and impaling it on his sword.

The combination of its imbalance and weight were too much however, driving Bretran off the edge of the cliff. He toppled backward, the beast falling with him. Grath and Ulgoth, too, were on the very precipice.

Talina cried out, but there was no time to stop. Three of the Were-Men were already turning toward her and Cyrith, who still sat on Bretran's stallion, leaving five surrounding Grath and Ulgoth. Even as she watched, however, one of the five dodged just a bit too slowly and Ulgoth's staff cracked it across the head as he swept it around to block one of the others.

The three Were-Men began to run toward them and Talina whispered again to her mare, which set off running into the darkness, Cyrith and the stallion right behind.

As they raced away, Talina thought grimly of Malakai. She still wasn't quite certain what to think of the boy and what he had said, but she could not doubt the truth behind his words.

He was almost certainly still alive, but soon the Nameless One would be loose as well. She thought also of the prophecies. They had been missing two of their number —or possibly only one. What of that? She shook her head. There was no way to know.

The Nameless One would require months, perhaps turnings to build his power, to break free again. Malakai had not said how long they might have. There was time to raise an army and, maybe, to defeat the Nameless One. She thought of Bretran and the cliff, but she had Cyrith to look out for. The others would simply have to take care of themselves. Yes. There was time, but time made all the more precious by the gravity of the situation.

Epilogue

The old man paused for a long moment as if reflecting, then, seemingly returned to the present, said, "…and so you see. A strange story indeed, and one that I sometimes doubt the truth of."

There was a quiet gasp from the corner of the room and all three strangers' heads snapped around toward the sound. They rose, and two of them circled outward, one moving into the middle of the room, the other passing him to stand near the wall, so the three surrounded the patron who had gasped.

The inn had gone silent, and everyone huddled in their chairs, watching the three strangers with more than a little fear. "You see," the leader said, "we are searching for the two who escaped, for the story you told is true, old man, doubt it though you may." He slowly reached up and pulled back the hood on his cloak to expose a face twisted and deformed. Gleaming yellow eyes stared from sockets that seemed too small to hold them, while long, ivory fangs stained yellow in places protruded from between his lips.

Gasps went up around the room, and the inn's patrons cowered in their seats as the other two strangers followed their leader's example, revealing faces equally hideous. The two people at the table in the corner stood up and drew back against the wall, their hoods pulled low so their faces couldn't be seen. The three Were-Men reached inside their cloaks and drew swords.

The beasts' leader said, "You! Remove your hoods so we may see who you are."

Slowly, the taller of the two figures removed his hood. As his face came into the light, they saw that it was a man so old his wrinkles piled up under his proud, frightened eyes and around his face like the weathered ridges and crags of a mountain. His beard was pure white. The smaller figure, seeing what the older had done, followed his example. It was a boy who looked to be about ten turnings old with a frightened, yet somehow defiant look.

A snarl with the undertones of a curse escaped the leader's lips, and the other two clamped their hands reflexively on their swords. He stared at the two for a long moment then a low, evil chuckle escaped his lips and he raised the hand not holding his sword.

The sinister wolf-man pointed two fingers at them and a beam of yellow light flowed from his hand to touch each of their faces in turn. The mask of light covering their faces melted into nothing, leaving behind a young girl and a woman so beautiful her face seemed to shine. Her pointed ears and aristocratic features were out of place above plain gray robes. The girl was small with short red hair and fine features. The change had been so complete that the only thing remaining of their former appearances was their eyes.

The leader chuckled again. "You've led us quite a merry chase, elf. Now it is time to finish what was started at the Black Lord's mountain two moons ago."

Before the three could start forward however, the sound of a sword being drawn came from the opposite corner of the room near the door. The Were-Men's heads turned, and suddenly Cyrith's hand was moving, pulling something out of her sleeve and sending it flying through the air. A moment later a knife buried itself in the throat of the creature next to the wall. As the dying beast clutched his throat, gurgling and trying to pull out the dagger, the leader turned to face the new danger, a man in a dirty brown cloak who moved quickly between tables toward the center of the room. The two remaining creatures started forward, one toward the girl and the elf, the other toward the man, both with swords raised, but the chair in which the leader had been sitting tipped over and he tripped on it, twisting in the air trying to land on his feet. He might have succeeded except that the old man's tobacco-stained pipe skittered out of nowhere to land beneath his descending foot. As the foot came down on the pipe, it turned, and the beastman went off balance again, falling headfirst into the fire.

Then came such an unearthly shriek as to make all the people in the inn cover their ears in pain. It rang through the room as the creature writhed on the hearth, half his face blackened by the fire and one yellow eye staring and sightless, embers sticking into the black mask that had been flesh. The other beastman's head snapped around to see what had happened to his leader, and the man in the brown cloak brought his sword around, cleaving his head from his shoulders.

While it was still falling, the man turned toward the leader, writhing on the hearth. Before he could start toward the creature however, he rose with a howl of rage and pain and fled toward the door, sword still in hand. Instead of opening the door though, the beast smashed it from its hinges and battered it to the ground outside the inn, and, still running, disappeared into the night.

In the wake of the creature's panicked departure, Bretran walked over to the doorway and stared thoughtfully into the darkness for a moment. Shrugging, he picked up the door and pulled it back into the frame as squarely as possible. Then he turned back into the room and strode toward the corner where Talina and Cyrith stood. Cyrith gave a cry and ran to him. He swept her up in a hug then set her back on her feet and bowed slightly to Talina.

She nodded, frowning, and said in her clear, musical voice, "Why have you waited so long to show yourself? It has been nearly a month. More than once we found sign in the forest, but..."

He scowled in the direction of the door. "When I fell down that cliff I landed in a pile of snow—atop that beast, thankfully. Soft snow, so I didn't break any bones, but the fall knocked me out. When I woke I tried to dig myself out. Couldn't.

"Grath and Ulgoth found me." He grimaced again, embarrassed at the memory. "By the time we found the trail, we were a day behind, without a horse. Two weeks after we started on your trail, I found their tracks." He jerked a thumb toward the dead beastman on the floor. "We followed them." He grimaced. "I lost them yesterday, so I found you two before they could." Talina nodded thoughtfully.

Cyrith was biting her lip, standing beside Talina's chair, and she said, "I thought you were dead. Talina said she would know, but when you fell...after Malakai..." she trailed off, tears coming to her eyes, and Bretran smiled gently at her, the hard planes of his face softening.

"Couldn't leave you alone, could I?" His lips curved into something half wry and half annoyed, and he broke his customary silence again to add, "Malakai bid me take care of you. He'd take it hard if I didn't, eh?" She nodded, still sniffling.

After a moment, Talina raised one eyebrow. "What of the others?"

Bretran's mouth quirked and he jerked a thumb to the south. "Grath got chewed on. Ulgoth had to carry him. They're camped down there." He grinned unexpectedly, then imitated Grath's voice. "Big bag of wind talk less walk more. Grath crawl faster than big oaf walk."

The three sat down, leaving the rest of the inn's occupants alternately darting glances at them and staring wide-eyed at the dead Beastmen on the floor, now twisted in their half-man, half-beast death rictus.

All except for the old man, who had retrieved his pipe from the floor where he tossed it and, after looking at it with obvious amusement, clamped it still unlit back in his jaws. He stared thoughtfully at the dead Beastman then glanced over to the table in the corner. For a moment the wrinkles melted from his face as he smiled, then he frowned slightly and stared again at the dead creature, now rapidly crumbling to dust on the floor.

If anyone had watched, they might have seen the youth that momentarily peeked from behind his aged countenance during that smile. No one had however, and as the last of the Changer's remains dispersed into the dirt of the floor, he sighed and closed his eyes, dozing again in the rickety chair beside the fire. Outside, the storm beat more fiercely than ever against the old inn, and the wind sent its chill howls into the winter darkness.

The keening wind blew long and hard
that bitter, frosty night,
to pierce the heart and chill the bone
and chase away the light.
When in the blasted land it claimed
the darkness woke once more,
To rend a battered world from which
'twas bound in time of yore.

Character Roster

Black Lord [Black Lord]: Mode of address used by followers of Sheklah to refer to it. *(See Sheklah)*

Byzimyanny [Buy-zim-yannee]: Term used by the Aylves to refer to Sheklah. *(See Sheklah)*

Bretran [Bre-tran]: Primary companion of Lady Talina of the Aylves, Speculation: May be the "Scion of Watchmen Bright" referred to in the prophecies of Eschaton.

> *Race* - Deegani

> *History* - Son of the King of Degan, in succession for the throne of Degan.

> *Allegiance* - King of Yore

Cyrith [Si-rith]: May be the "child of dwarves and fairies" referred to in the prophecies of Eschaton.

> *Race* - Fae *(Dwarf/Fairie)*

> *History* - Castoff of the Wild Hunt. History unknown.

> *Allegiance* - King of Yore

Degahyaso [Day-gah-yah-sow]: Term used by the Simianites *(trolls)* to refer to Sheklah. *(See Sheklah)*

Gan-Anym [Gan-anim]: Term used by the Gygans *(giants)* to refer to Sheklah. *(See Sheklah)*

Grath [Grath]: Speculation: May be the "son of fallen Simia" of the prophecies of Eschaton.

Race - Simianite *(troll)*

History - First encountered in the cave at the entrance to Sheklah's cavern complex.

Allegiance - King of Yore

Great Wizard (of Yore) [Grate-Wizerd]: Liegeman of the King of Yore, Major figure in the history of Eschaton.

Race - Unknown

History - Conflicting reports as to origin. Defeated Sheklah, the nameless, in the Battle of Ages.

Allegiance - King of Yore

King of Yore [King-Uv-Yor]: The ruler of the world in the time before Sheklah and the Battle of Ages.

Race - Unknown

History - Unknown

Allegiance - Unknown

Malakai [Ma-la-kye]: Companion of Cyrith, also liegeman and messenger to the King of Yore.

Race - Deegani *(Presumed)*

History - Presumably raised (or at least sheltered by) the Fae. Unusual for a Deegani.

Allegiance - King of Yore

Nameless One [Naym-less Won]: Term used by the Deegani to refer to Sheklah. *(See Sheklah)*

Nyvtelen [Niv-te-len]: Term used by the Theurgans *(wizard race)* to refer to Sheklah. *(See Sheklah)*

Old Man [Ohld - Man]: Storyteller at the Inn.

    Race - Deegani *(Presumed)*

    History - Unknown

    Allegiance - Unknown

Sheklah [Shek-law]: The proper name of the evil being who rose up in opposition to the King of Yore in the age of Yore.

    Race - Unknown

    History - Conflicting reports as to origin. Lost to the Great Wizard of Yore in the Battle of Ages. Was presumably imprisoned in The North thereafter.

    Allegiance - Unknown

Talina [Ta-lee-nuh]: Speculation: May be the "Princess of the Woodlands" referred to in the prophecies of Eschaton.

    Race - Aylf

    History - World traveler. Assured by her people that she would never be an elder of the Talonwood.

    Allegiance - King of Yore

Ulgoth [Uhl-goth]: Speculation: May be the "son of fallen Simia" of the prophecy of Eschaton

    Race - Gygan

    History - First encountered in the cave at the entrance to Sheklah's cavern complex.

    Allegiance - King of Yore

Ynaithnid [In-ayth-nid]: Term used by the Fae *(dwarves and fairies)* to refer to Sheklah. *(See Sheklah)*

Ynami [In-am-ee]: Term used by the Changers *(were-men)* to refer to Sheklah. *(See Sheklah)*

Glossary

Aylves [Ale-vz]: One of the seven races of men. Long-lived, but slow to reproduce. Clan-like, almost tribal society.

Also known as: Elves *(commonly)*

Battle of Ages [Bad-dle uv Ajes]: The battle waged long ago between the Great Wizard and Sheklah the Nameless that resulted in Sheklah's defeat and presumable imprisonment.

Book of Yore [Buk uv Your]: The book of wisdom and prophecy left by the Wizard before his disappearance to guide the world in his absence.

Cataclysm [Cat-uh-cli-zum]: The ancient event that divided both the land of Eschaton and its people, originally the great Sidhe, into the seven races of men.

Changer [Chain-jer]: One of the seven races of men. Able to shape-shift into other forms, such as *(commonly)* wolves.

Also known as: Half-men, Were-men, etc.

Daemons [Day-muns]: Magical beings that once originated as Engyls, now twisted to the service of their master, Sheklah.

Dark Hounds [Dark Hownds]: Companion beasts of the Fae, only rarely seen by other races of man, usually during the Wild Hunt.

Degan [Day-gon]: One of the seven races of men. Short-lived, industrious and fecund. Tend toward feudal or imperial political structures.

Plural: **Deegani [Day-gon-ee]**

Also: The primary political unit of the race of Degan, an empire.

Dragon [Dra-gun]: A mysterious flying lizard beast, known for great age, wisdom, and sometimes treachery.

Dread Steed [Dred Steed]: Companion mounts of the Fae, only rarely seen by other races of man, usually during the Wild Hunt.

Elf [Elf]: *(See Aylves)*

Engyl [En-gill]: A magical being, often tasked with the oversight of elemental forces. Possessing free will and often great intelligence and power. Usually bound to a particular area.

Eschaton [Es-kuh-tawn]: The world upon which the events of Winternight take place.

Fae [Fay]: One of the seven races of men. Most known for digging and underground exploration. Tend toward dynastic or familial political structures *(extended clans).*

Also known as: Fair Folk, Dwarves, Fairies

Findale [Fin-dayle]: A small city on the outskirts of the Empire of Degan.

Gargyl [Gar-gill]: A magical entity of unknown properties and temperament. Purportedly worse than Daemons.

Grand Gorge [Grand gorj]: An independent, multi-ethnic port city of traders and merchants.

Great Oath [Grayt Ohth]: A direct magical binding mysteriously connected with the forces of creation. Those who swear by it are bound beyond their ability to resist. *(See Old Magic.)*

Gygans [Guy-gans]: One of the seven races of men. Most known for their great size and passion for creating megalithic structures. Tend toward democratic or republican political structures.

 Also known as: Giants

Half-men [Haf men]: *(See Changer)*

Links [Linkz]: Unit of measurement *(just under a foot).*

Madra'risa [Mah-draw-ree-suh]: The black mountains of The North *(See North, the)* under which Sheklah the nameless was long thought to be imprisoned.

North, the [North]: The area traditionally held to be the original domain of Sheklah, now covered in mostly-uninhabited dark forest.

Old Magic [Old Majik]: Forces of creation that are poorly understood, governed by strict rules that may not be broken, but often displaying very little visible power until those rules are challenged.

Prophecies of Eschaton [Praw-fu-seez uv Es-kuh-tawn]: Writings from the Book of Yore that predict the future of Eschaton, including the Reckoning.

Races of Man [Rasus uv Man]: The seven different races descended from the Sidhe, the eighth and original race. *See: Aylves, Changers, Deegani, Fae, Gygans, Simianites, and Theurgans*

Reckoning [Wreck-un-ing]: Fabled time of judgment, during which the races of man will be united and the King of Yore will return to mete out justice to everyone, great and small.

Sidhe [She]: The original, unblemished race of man from before the Cataclysm. Characteristics and tendencies only rumored.

Simia [Si-me-uh]: One of the seven races of men. Short-lived, brutish and often considered stupid by the other races. Reproduce VERY quickly. Political tendencies unknown (because they've always been enslaved).

Plural: **Simianites [Si-me-uh-nites]**

Also known as: *Trolls*

Star of Yore [Star uv Your]: A powerful magical artifact originally emplaced as a seal within the mountains of the north, to hold back the power of Sheklah. Presumably keeping him bound in his prison.

Theurgans [Thur-guns]: One of the seven races of men. Long-lived, reclusive, and power-hungry. Barely able to reproduce. Political tendencies unknown.

Also known as: Wizards

Troll [Trohl]: *(See Simia)*

Turning [Turn-ing]: A unit of time measurement. Analogous to (but not necessarily equal to) a year.

Watchmen: [Wotsh-mun]: *(See Degan)*

Were-men [Where men]: *(See Changer)*

Wild Hunt [Wyld Hunt]: A traditional Fae event, used as both a social outing and a defensive/offensive strategic activity.

Winternight [Win-tur-night]: A day of power, when all the known magical forces of the world are more active and available.

Yore [Your]: A time from before the Cataclysm, when the world was young, inhabited by the Sidhe and directly governed by the King of Yore.

About the Author

© 2023 - Rachel Collins Photography LLC

Jared N. Michaud is a devoted fiction writer driven by a passion for writing that began before he reached age seven. Influenced by literary giants like C.S. Lewis and Orson Scott Card, he discovered the power of storytelling, and at twelve he began crafting his first novel.

Today, Jared writes from a little house in a little town in Wyoming, where he lives with his wife and seven children. As a Christian with a deep love for the truth and appreciation for the values that underlie Western civilization, he endeavors to create myths that will inspire future generations.

An Excerpt From
Il Alka E'Talania
(The Path of the Talonwood)
Mythologia - Book 2

Talina rode her mare stiffly, irritation overcoming her usually-good horsemanship as her mind was busy far away. Talina was not normally the type to brood, but she was as close to brooding as she had ever been. The Deegani and their petty politics might just turn a routine succession into the end of the world. She let out a half-bitter, half-ironic snort and shifted a bit in her saddle. ...Quite literally the end of the world.

She'd known Deegani were stubborn and self-centered, but the situation in Degan was so ridiculous it might have been amusing in other circumstances. As it was, the situation preyed upon her mind. Bretran's half-brother, the fool Aratan, would have to wake up with a daemon standing over his bed before he took any notice of the parts of the world that did not orbit him.

She had never thought it would be easy when they returned from the Madra'risa with news of the Nameless One's awakening. Telling the world of what happened there on Winternight would be like trying to get a room full of trolls to do magic. Though they had learned the Nameless One was still alive and seen his daemons face to face, it would take miracles to convince their respective peoples.

They had only escaped from the great cavern above the Nameless One's prison with the help of Malakai, a messenger from... Talina shook her head. Could it really be the King of Yore?

She had sworn allegiance to the King, as her people traditionally did when they came of age. Her people were the exception, however. By most races' reckoning, the King was dead, gone from Eschaton forever, or some sort of distant, uncaring deity, and certainly not a living man as Malakai had said. ...And for all she knew, Malakai was dead —though she suspected he was too cunning to die so easily. More likely, he was either caught by the Nameless One's minions or gone to a place only he knew.

The battle he fought under the Madra'risa, the black northern mountains, was beyond her comprehension. She was no sage; her ability with magic came in fits and starts. Her peoples' own greatest wise ones and sages could do nothing to help her with her abilities. In fact, they had never seen anyone with power as strange or temperamental as hers. Despite all that, she could always tell when someone was using magic—and she could sense, more or less, how much they used. Talina had seen powerful sages at work more than once, but the energies she felt washing over her that night under the Madra'risa were far more than she had ever conceived of, and even now she could scarcely believe what she had seen there. After they escaped from the hellish, black cavern, they rode back to Bretran's home, following a final encounter with some of the Nameless One's minions.

That, of course, was when she met Aratan, Bretran's half brother and the favorite to succeed his father to the throne. He had been oh-so-polite, even when they announced their finds in the North, then ignored them as much as possible. "Plenty of room for all in The North," he'd said lightly, pretending to jest while mocking laughter danced in his eyes. Talina could have spat. In his face. Nothing was more disgusting than a patronizing Deegani with a swollen head!

As Talina's mind ran back through the same loop she had been worrying at for the past week, a part of her still watched the world around. She was an Aylf, a creature of the forest. She had been born in the very forest through which she traveled, and she spent the first years of her life learning its ways. The forest was her home, and she knew it well.

Even so, she never consciously realized what alerted her. It could have been a tiny sound, perhaps a movement, or even mere instinct, but one moment she was sitting upright in her saddle, replaying the same stale thoughts, and the next, totally without conscious thought, she had flung herself to one side and hit the ground, rolling into the brush.

The arrow meant for her thudded into her saddle, but she didn't have time to think of anything except her attacker. Where was he? Her eyes raked the forest...there! The black-clad figure knelt on the branch of a tree and pulled another arrow to his cheek, then loosed, already flinging himself forward off the branch to fall through the air toward her. Talina rolled to her feet and felt the wind of his arrow tickle her ear.

Another arrow buried itself in a tree a hand's breadth from her head as she dodged through the brush, and she stole a glance behind. Her pursuer was as quick and silent as she. She could see him, ducking around bushes behind her. Turning to fight never crossed her mind. She had little training with a sword or knife, and didn't even carry one except her hunting knife. She was capable enough with a bow, but hers was on her horse. Besides, she had suspicions about what her pursuer might be and no desire to find out. At best he was an assassin, and much as it horrified her, she could tell from the way he moved that he was probably another elf. At worst... Visions of the dark creatures in those horrible northern caverns she had so recently escaped flashed through her mind.

The worst didn't bear thinking about.

Talina stole another glance behind her. She was gaining ground, but she had to lose him. Talina spotted thick brush ahead and to the left and swerved suddenly, putting a giant Talonwood tree between herself and her pursuer. Then she threw herself head-first into a hole in the bushes. She landed and rolled to one side. There were no thorns she noted thankfully as she lay still, barely breathing. Her heartbeat sounded loud in her ears. She was starving for air, but she dared not breathe any louder. She heard only a whisper, like the slightest wind stirring the leaves as he ran past. His feet whispered over the forest floor like a breeze, and his movement through the brush disturbed nothing. Such skill could come only from long practice.

Quickly, knowing she had little time, Talina stood and stepped to the bole of a tree. For a choking moment, she fought against panic and helplessness. Once her pursuer discovered he'd lost her, he would return to hunt her trail. All elves were trained in the ways of the forest to a greater or lesser degree. Even a child could follow its creatures by the sign they left behind. There were few trails that could be hidden entirely, and the thicker the forest the fewer they were.

Then she willed herself back to calm and purpose. She had learned the best ways to fool a tracker, and there was only one rule: do the unexpected. There were, of course, small tricks she could use, ways to hide the marks she left behind her on the ground, but she had the sinking feeling that the trail she left behind would not be her undoing.

The lore of the Aylves, the tradition and collective wisdom of her people, taught another, more important trail: "Il alka e'cathri"—the path of the mind. To find the body, follow the mind. Know the objective, see the path. The question was where her pursuer would expect her to go.

Likely he would expect her to go back for her horse. By now Aolaira was long gone, headed for home without her. She had trained the mare well. If she was within a hundred leagues of home and fell from the saddle, Aolaira would go home without her—which, ironically, reduced her possible destinations to one. It was a three-day walk to Estaria, and she could not afford to lose time.

She must go home, and home was the second place her pursuer would look for her. She could not do the unexpected. The best she could do would be to take a roundabout route and still get there as quickly as possible. Simply striking out for home would likely be fatal. He would find and follow her trail far too easily. As she leaned against the bole of the old tree for a moment, considering, Talina took in the air and the spirit of the forest that was her peoples' ancient home. It had been too long since she visited.

The forest where she now stood was the Talonwood. More to the point, it was the only place where the great Talonwood trees grew. They were huge, many hundreds of links high with several levels of branches, growing much closer together than should have been possible for such giants and creating several levels of interweaving branches that in ancient times had functioned as arboreal highways.

Of late, the elves had taken to walking the ground as the surrounding races did. Horses had provided a huge advance in how quickly the elves could travel, and the elves had tried for many years to train their mounts to walk among the great Talonwoods. They had failed every time—often spectacularly. So, the elves who used the Talonwood highways had become nearly as scarce as those who still spoke more than snippets of their ancient language. She could count the ones who did so frequently on her fingers.

That arboreal legacy would be her escape.

A short while later, Talina was jogging easily along, hundreds of links above the forest floor, pacing herself carefully. It was several leagues yet until she reached her destination, and leaving sign, even here, could easily be fatal. Nor were the Talonwood roads themselves particularly safe—another reason they were perfect for her purposes.

A sudden thought gave Talina a little short-lived relief. When Aolaira arrived without her, her family would surely begin a search for her. Activity could frighten her pursuer off. If she could reach home, the assassin might think twice before attacking. Her brothers were much more skilled with bow and sword than she, and they would not take kindly to someone trying to harm her. ...But she still had to get there, and if she didn't hurry the assassin could precede her.

Hours later, long after night had fallen, Talina lay upon the branch of a great Talonwood on the edge of the meadow surrounding her family's home. The meadow was one of those rare clearings that exist for no obvious reason in the middle of the forest. Instead of thinning out, the forest ended abruptly, giving way to a grassy hill upon which her distant ancestors had built their home. All around the clearing towered the Talonwood, the wall of greenery higher than the clearing was wide, and it was within this wall of living forest the killer would have to hide. If he was there, lying in wait, he would try to finish her as she crossed the clearing.

She saw no sign of her would-be killer during her trek through the branches of the Talonwood, however, and she had lain upon her perch for over an hour now, watching for any signs of wrongness around her. There were none, and she was nearly certain he wasn't lurking anywhere near.

Slowly, still scanning her surroundings, Talina began to descend. When she reached the ground, she gave one long look around then stepped from the forest and strode toward the house. Her instinct was to run for the house and shelter, but something in her balked. Running from shadows showed weakness, and she was no mouse... Besides, she thought, her lips twisting ironically, considering the skill her assassin had shown, it would make little difference anyway. On her way to the house, Talina neither hurried nor looked over her shoulder, but her back hunched in anticipation of the arrow she half expected to come hurtling out of the darkness. No arrow came.

As she approached, however, the focus of her attention turned from the forest around her to the buildings, and she gasped aloud. In all the time she watched for her assassin, she had somehow neglected to study the house closely, and now it was obvious to her that something was very wrong. The house was dark, not particularly odd for so late at night, but there was a stillness to it that was... out of place. The stables too were quiet, for one, and Talina felt a finger of dread creeping up her back as she hurried to the door.

When she opened it, the smell stopped her as suddenly as if she had run into a stone wall. It was a smell of wrongness, of a dark evil that set her teeth on edge and made her stomach hollow. That scent had first come to her in the black northern mountains, in the same woods where she and her companions fled for their lives from the Nameless One's pursuing minions.

The smell was as foreign to nature as it was possible to be—the ancient, fetid stench of the perverted land that had once belonged to the Nameless One. Only two thousand turnings before, his warped magic had corrupted the people and creatures of the land he ruled into an army of hate-consumed demons. Some were taken against their will and twisted into malformed things—tortured and repulsive, desiring only their own deaths. Others... others had been his willing tools, and those he had remade—stretching and reshaping the bodies and souls of men and animals alike until they became his minions, remade to pollute and destroy the rest of creation.

Talina's eyes worked nearly as well in the darkness as in sunlight, so she could see everything as she opened the door and gazed into the room. Nothing inside moved, and nothing seemed out of place...except a dark mound in the center of the entry-hall floor. It looked like... oh dear light!

Talina stepped forward and knelt, her heart skipping wildly. She reached out and slowly drew aside the cloak hiding the corpse's face.

It was her sister, Estella. Half of her face was gone, torn away, and what remained shone a sickly green. The wound was black and jagged, and the smell of poisonous death hung about her.

Talina leapt to her feet, her stomach trying to empty itself, mind rebounding in shock and pain. The move probably saved her life. As her head came up, she caught sight of two glowing red eyes in the shadows at the end of the entry hall.

The smell of twisted wrongness increased three-fold, and Talina reached blindly for the rack beside the door where her family kept the walking staves. The staves were specially formed from the seasoned wood of the oak trees that grew at the outskirts of the Talonwood. Most were hundreds of years old, and they had been used as weapons on more than one occasion.

Staring down the hall, Talina knew she would need the best weapon she could lay hand to. In front of her, a creature slowly emerged from the shadows. It had a cat-like frame covered completely in fine, black fur, ending in a tail tipped with a dagger-like sting. Talina's people did not purposefully teach their children about the Nameless One's creatures, but many of their legends and fables were based on the time of the Great War. If Talina's memory served her as well as usual, the creature's tail and claws carried deadly venom.

The Bastithria's red eyes were already focused on her, and it stalked forward another pace. It was beautiful in a terrible, twisted way.

No. It might have been breathtakingly beautiful, had it not been twisted into a foul mockery of beauty. Its streamlined body was designed for the pursuit and destruction of anything lesser—over land or through the trees. It seemed that it might move unpredictably, faster than sight like a striking snake, and looking at it left no doubt of the latent power in its wiry muscles. Then its mouth opened and an unearthly screech filled the hall.

Baring its fangs, it leaped forward almost too fast for her to register. Talina threw herself back out the door a split second before the beast's fangs closed where her shoulder had been. Her staff came up and she struck at it. Her blow caught nothing but air, and she was barely able to bring up her staff around to block the next lightning-swift strike from its paw. She didn't dare take even a flesh wound. Those teeth and claws were as poisonous as the tail that now whipped at her.

Talina never remembered how she survived the next few minutes. She only knew that she and the creature fought in circles in front of her family's home for seconds that were days to her. She became more and more desperate as the battle continued. She was beginning to tire, and she didn't dare turn to run. The thing was more agile in the trees than on the ground. She had nowhere to retreat other than the house, and who knew what else might be inside?

Moments later, Talina found herself backed against a wall with the creature poised for a final leap. She slid sideways, trying to escape, and stumbled backward through the doorway. The creature changed direction to follow her, and she threw her staff at it. The two met in mid air, and the Bastithria swatted the staff aside with the sweep of a paw, landing directly in front of her. Talina backed up frantically and tripped over her sister's sprawled body.

The creature hissed and spat as it stalked forward, stepping casually onto Estella, and Talina felt her eyes filling with tears of pain, sorrow... and rage as she held her torn arm to her chest—an arm that she could not remember hurting. No, no, NO! This could NOT happen! She would NOT die on a cold floor to this gods-blighted creature! It killed her family, but it would NOT kill her. Not now. She could not leave her people, unsuspecting, directly in the Nameless One's path. Talina's rage built until a red haze formed in front of her eyes.

Curiously, in what must be her last moments, her mind seemed to retreat within her to all the times she had shared with her family and to growing up in the Talonwood. She remembered her first climb, the hours she had spent learning the ancient "il alka le'Enai," the ways of the forest, and elf lore. It had all come to this. Her life was done, her message still undelivered. It was NOT right!

The Bastithria crouched, its tail poised to strike, and Talina cried out in despair and frustration, screaming words that she would not remember until much later, "Eanai! Eanai! Eanai al e'Ayaia! Tarios il Madradaria! Bicole Eanai o'Talania!" With her utterance, the creature hesitated, as if in surprise. Then, a moment later, it froze completely, its body totally still except for its terrible eyes, which darted side to side. With a howl it shrank back from her, eyes rolling in what was unmistakably fear. Then, turning, it leaped out the door, fleeing for the forest. Halfway across the clearing, something seized the creature mid-leap and pulled it violently to earth. Screaming in pain, it writhed and howled, dark vines like coarse ropes reaching from the ground to ensnare it and pull it down. Soon one limb was caught, then another. Before long, the

Bastithria was pinned completely. Then the writhing mass, now more vine than beast, began to contract. From her half-reclined sprawl, propped on one arm in the entry hall of her parents' house, Talina heard bones snap. One final anguished scream filled the air, tearing at the last of her sanity, and there was silence.

The forest, however, was not done. The mass of vines continued to writhe long after Talina had blacked out from pain, exhaustion, and relief.